Choosing Spectacles

Choosing Spectacles

ROSALIND BELBEN

'The Permit to Wake Up' first appeared in *Stand Magazine*, and the chapter 'Choosing Spectacles' in *Active in Airtime*: to the respective editors all due acknowledgement.

The author thanks the Authors' Foundation for a grant received in 1989.

Set in 10.5pt Caslon 540
Printed in Finland by Werner Söderström Oy

contents

Choosing Spectacles

the permit to wake up

I dreamt we had to have a permit to wake up, and that each time we went to sleep it had to be renewed, had to be applied for again, and that there would be a painful wait, on an uncomfortable chair perhaps, or in a queue in heavy rain, before the necessary piece of paper was produced, handed, that is, through a tiny window in a blank wall or passed from hand to hand in a badly-lit corridor. But I had no business to be dreaming this.

I wake sometimes and the bed is all flung about, the lamp knocked over, in my sleep I may have been trying to light a glass of water, thinking it a torch and the batteries hopelessly run down, or I may have been striking matches on the ashtray and holding them to a damp candle, and there will be water on the floor or in the mattress and tooth-paste, my candle, spread on the pillow.

I dreamt of a book; of a bookshop in which there were perhaps nine or ten volumes laid out on a counter and a handful more displayed on shelving behind the assistants. A bookshop with exceedingly few books in it. At the assis-tants' feet, and for every three books there was one assistant, at their feet stood parcels, sealed inside thick brown paper and stout string, not the wrapping paper and string one could buy, that wrapping paper was purple. A queue had formed. It was early in the morning. At least two assistants looked nervous. In bookshops there were always assistants who looked nervous, and for every nervous-looking assistant two more merely nervous, or not merely. In bookshops everybody could be afraid. The queue had formed because customers filled the shop, leaning against the counter, trying to squint over to the other side, and pressing against the tasselled rope which kept them away from certain spaces in the shop. Customers overwhelmed already by anxiety and despair, and by curiosity. It was first thing in the morning and the new parcels had arrived. Hungry eyes followed the parcels from the door to the floor behind the counter, drinking them in. The queue heaved and craned. An assistant very slowly, tantalisingly, undid the string round one parcel, and stopped. She moved away, abandoning the parcel. She didn't smile. The customers might not for her have been there. That wasn't her fault. The assistants drifted assid-uously about, doing invisible chores. The breath of the people crushed against the counter poured over their legs as they passed. The people could see the parcels through the assistants' invisible legs. Past the door, past the out-of-door part of the queue, office-workers were still speeding. It was chilly. The collective breath of the queue hung in the air. I too was anxious for a book to arrive, but in my dream I couldn't remember which book it was, I would know it when I saw it, when the brown paper came off and a single copy was laid face up on the rest. The queue shifted ground. Young lady! called an old man in a sweet tone. The assistant peered under the counter. A moment of bustle. Someone lifted the bandage, the brown paper. A gasp. Hands, palms down, and chests were pressed flat on the broad counter, too broad. The excitement mounted and then billowed a little and sank. It was not what we were hoping for. In my dream I didn't know what we were hoping for. It was the second volume of the translation of Proust's *À la recherche du temps perdu*. The assistants handed out book after book. The customers struggled to seize their slips of paper for the cashier, struggled to make their way to the cashier, struggled with a fresh slip back, and when their fingers touched their books their faces subsided with relief. The assistants took their time, twisting a leaf of crumbly paper and a rubber band round each purchase. In a matter of minutes, though, the lot was snapped up. The brown wrapping vanished too. The eagerness of that particular day was over. I stood desolate outside the bookshop's window with my back to the everlasting thoughts in it.

But I had no business to be dreaming this.

My young brother was doodling. In the sky, in the dream, a rainbow, seen through the classroom window. He was doodling on an old newspaper, on a face, a picture of someone, faces attract doodlers, they are natural magnets, better a face than, say, a tractor, or vast horizons of sunflowers, a face with no moustache, no sticky-out ears, no funny eyebrows, a face, a plain face. The pencil moved, the teacher burbled on, she was trying hard not to drone, she wasn't a bad teacher, my brother was trying hard, he took in what she was telling them, the good teacher who was trying not to drone, better if he doodled, doodling helped, and she was unruffled by it. And already the moustache was waxy and big, the eyebrows were beginning to be sinister, the lips swelled and at the corners cynically curled, an ear was mis-shapen, some very accomplished wrinkles and a small insect crossed the forehead, and my little brother hasn't noticed what face it is he's drawing on, whose face, the face of somebody far from gaga, my brother's thoughts are for the doodling and the teacher's voice, and it is over, the class is, the lesson taught, he floods out in the wake of the teacher with the other children, the doodle stays behind on his desk, the cleaner comes in at the end of the day and the next morning the cleaner denounces him to the teacher, it would be the cleaner. The teacher was presented by the cleaner with the doodle, the disfigured face, and although the teacher was kind and sensible and would rather by far have thought nothing more of it she was too scared to do anything but denounce him, my young brother, she felt forced to, or she may even have been forced to, kindliness is nothing to confront fear with, private promptings are nothing, she denounced him, in my dream, higher up. So a level-headed boy knew terror, possibly well-justified, possibly not, who could tell. He went home. He sat on his bed. He wrote me a letter. It was found in his pocket. He wrote to me, his big brother, far away, a letter which explained what he'd done, how he'd doodled without noticing whose face he was doodling on, he explained it all briefly and to the point. The rainbow had certainly gone and it was towards dusk. He walked out of the house. Out of the little town, and into the little wood. Beyond the edge of the wood he met a good, kindly tree from which to hang himself. Then he hanged himself. His teacher cried for two days, but privately. She dared not let the cleaner see her tears; she said, she had a stye threatening. But I had no business to dream this.

One thinks one can't recover, one may say it very privately perhaps, then one goes about and time passes and one seems to cope, if badly, but it is true, it was true, it has been true all along, one can't recover, and one hasn't, and will not, ever. It is like trying to live without someone one loves and without whom too much is lost, someone who is, though, alive, alive somewhere, unattainable: like the inverse of that.

A sick analogy.

I have no business to wake up.

I feel like a snake, trying to swallow a much too large rabbit, deathly tired.

She writes to me that she is ill, then nothing, nothing more, for a long time; simply, she is ill, she is going to see a doctor, then after a long time has passed, and nothing, again, she is ill, the doctor is seeing her. I ask what I should send, medicines, what in the way of those, and she replies that there is no need, no need for a leg of lamb, or of beef, it tells me she isn't waiting for an operation, no one has demanded something absurd of her to cut a piece of her out.

Then, I think, I realised I didn't know if she were dead or alive. I had to put my one foot after the other, wake, sleep, open my mouth, shut my mouth, smile, pull money out of my pocket, not having news, with no telephone connection, certain, when it came, if it came, the news would be old news, that much might have happened since, there was nothing I could do, many people suffered a lack of news, patient, tense, one had to see it made no difference, it was a purely subjective, selfish need, to know if someone lives still or lies dead or is badly ill, the turmoil within one is pointless indulgence, one has to give the possibility its head and not fret, it is a pathetic feeling, to be sure, a leg-of-mutton feeling.

One asks, what is it. The kidneys, she says. I've been dialling our number for two hours, before a line is granted us, the dialling exhausts one, she could ring from the street and doesn't. What's up with the kidneys. How could you leave us, she says.

In a moment of thoughtlessness, it seems, I have.

I said, hoping to make a joke, so we might talk a little lightly for a change, I tried, you know, earlier, to put my cup full of coffee on my nose instead of my spectacles, or over my eyes, strain tells, so she says in a small voice, you have coffee, you have coffee to put on your nose, and she makes it a question, unbarbed, *our* noses, she says, and tails away... But they too must have coffee, unless it didn't arrive, excellent coffee.

I have nights of banging and twisting my head on the pillow. Treading hard on a savage tooth. Kidneys, she says. Bring your kidneys and come. How, she answers. And then silence.

It was the innocent thoughtlessness of someone by turns overwrought and exhausted.

One doesn't just pay for happiness, one pays for unhappiness too.

I am writing in the belief that you are ill and you hear me yet, that you are there. The telephone is too terrible, because we can't speak, to speak to each other is overwhelming; with such excitement and such agitation one is unable to cope; it is better not to try, to talk and have to refrain from saying what is to be said ... I meant, to have to encode all we wished to say to each other... it's too much, so rather not. Please know I didn't leave you. I had the chance and took it, in the belief that you would follow. Easier for you to, once I am gone, by a long chalk. I never guessed that you would be ill in the meantime. I didn't plan it. Truly. If I'd had it worked out I'd have talked over every last detail with you. It was a flash of inspiration, which one obeys before one knows what is in store. I did not bring my winter great-coat. It still hangs with you. The hens do not lay so many eggs; clay, not silver. The language is unbearable, to be borne, however. If you need medicines you must tell me, I shall send whatever you desire. I am very alone and one is not so welcome. They are trained to make difficulties, to discourage a swarm. It is not as one imagined to oneself. Yet. Yet. So I kiss you both.

Poor words, but still words, which I crave also from you.

Once one has left one cannot go back. It is utterly beyond one, something beyond not courage but stomach, to go back, there is no stomach for it any more, as though the whole body revolts, hysterical.

I write a few lines concerning Amor. I write, there is a little boat called Amor. She has become familiar, to me a reassuring sight. She sleeps not here but in the heart of the city. I am glad to have a friend. Hard to imagine a boat for a friend. I write about other affairs, that was all I wrote concerning Amor. Then I posted the letter, without further thought.

Little Amor I know well. I know them all, but for little Amor I have affection. She is far from being the smartest, newest. She has no fancy trappings, no comforts. She is quite slow. If one watches the big ones, Sanssouci and Moby Dick, Großer Kurfürst, how they rip through the water, one says to oneself, little Amor is very slow. But to me she is pretty. When one is alone and has too much to think about, one can have a relationship with a boat. The thing about Amor is that one sees her in two different places. She doesn't live at the Wannsee mooring, several other boats do, she goes home every evening to the Landwehr Canal, to the Spree, she sleeps in the heart of the city and visits Wannsee in the hours of the day. It begins to touch me, when one has too much to think of, when the heart is heavy, and the mind recoils, when progress somewhere is essential, seeing her bow-wave, to see her moving sturdy and bustling, slow through the water, she at least doesn't drown. The heart stops, to see little Amor.

At the end of its journey, neither to Wannsee nor to the heart of the city, my letter reads, hotly decoded, differently. When one is used to it, decoding, when one is guarded by nature, one reads such a text with ease. This then is what my letter says to an inflamed and injured mind.

Look, there is a young girl. I have grown to know and to like her. She doesn't sleep at night with me but goes to her home in the city. I am glad to have a friend. Hard ... very hard ... to imagine having a German for a lover. I didn't realise my letter was revealing. She writes back to me:

I don't believe a word of it, concerning your friend Amor. You might be kind enough not to make up nonsense with which to torment me. How can I or you at such a moment be thinking of boats. I ask you not to be silly. There is not a jot of truth in it. I know you too well. You would never utter the language of the so-called Amor to Amor. Have done.

The next letter said:

I cannot put the boat out of my mind. Do not ever write to me again of boats.

The letter after that said:

You didn't receive my letter.

And then:

Tell me there is no truth in it, that you imagined it all. What do the boats float on.

I answer: I am far too weary to think of boats. The boat I wrote to you about is a real boat. She floats on water. It is lavish, and forests. I added, thoughtlessly, in the street in the city, in the Ku'damm, boats for hire, I find it rather refreshing and decadent, pretty boats, not very dressed, in

fisher boots. You'd be amazed. And in the streets away from
the thoroughfare, lacy stockings with hair from between the
legs combed out under black leaves and roses. Or more
probably look the other way.

And she writes:

You didn't receive my letter.

Next, tartly, I'd prefer it if you were in Venice.

For that matter, so should I.

Tell me you made it all up. I tell her I made it all up, it's
simpler; more tedious, a misunderstanding, to dispel, than a
fantasy.

Every day, such inanities ... But my fault.

I can't say the words she wants to hear, although they
would be true.

It is all quite bewildering, she writes, for you, and so
much more for us, when we can't be with you. So what, she
writes, if there are no tomatoes, one day there will be
tomatoes, though not, I begin to feel, for me, for me no
tomatoes.

Her despair is a broken umbrella which keeps collapsing
and the spokes go into one's eye and the eye waters indig-
nantly; and I don't have neat fingers.

She can't come with an illness she can't hide. I also can't
tell her. Even to be cured she can't come. Especially not to
be cured.

And when we telephone I can't speak, I don't find any
words to speak and I hurt her, horribly, precious minutes
with a connection on the telephone go by and I hear her
silence, or she fills it, unsure of herself, unsure of me,
instead of health insurance in the womb perhaps we have
the gift of being wounded, and we are to sit as snug with it,
the wound, as they with their insurance, free to be ill.

She is caught because she is. I have to explain, there is no insurance for what one already has, the insurance is for what one might have, for the health one comes with one pays, so if one is to arrive with poor health it has to be convincingly lied about, one has to be dishonest, it seems everyone is dishonest, if one isn't ready to be dishonest one doesn't have a life worth living, in exchange for poor health nothing. A hump, you know, is no good, the whole world notices the fib in it.

I have to ask what size I take, for shirts, for socks and trousers I don't dare. I have to ask her what they lack, I don't dare that either.

It isn't real, it isn't happening, she says. She forbears, she doesn't say, she doesn't beg me, start back at once.

I write to her, when we are cold and ill and without the necessary medicines, without an aspirin, and we are aware that aspirins are poured in millions elsewhere over the counter, it is a small jump to thinking that aspirins lead to more than aspirins, one has to set the health insurance off before one is born, in the womb, if it is to work, if it is to cover all feasible events, and it is anyway dear.

I explain, there is private, for which you pay, and there is the Krankenkasse, for which you also pay but if you can't then not or not so much, the people of the Krankenkasse employ a doctor to size you up and if you are already ill the doctor will say what risk you are, how much you will cost and together they decide whether they accept you or not, if you look expensive they don't take you, they turn you down, and you fend for yourself. It's the system.

Please don't tease me, she says. You must have laid plans, secretly. Without our knowledge, plans which didn't include us.

I am so far away, I write, and explanations so often make it worse. That, she says, is for us, I think, to decide. If you do what the you we know would never do, we may ask what possessed you. Is it important, I write. It is, she replies. To us.

And she writes, you are not to worry about us, we thank you for your parcel, I was a little poorly but now I am better. You should look after yourself and not fret. There is nothing else to be done and what you send in brown paper and string is more practical than what you send in a white envelope. We are not insulted by that in the brown yet sometimes by that which you put in the white.

I think I'd written, I feel close to you. I understand. I too am alone.

I have warmth, I have light, food I eat, food I buy, one shops with no great effort, I have insecurity, there is anxiety of an extreme sort.

I have applied, she says, confident.

Each time I went out of doors, or she did, I used to think, we may not see each other again, but this time, going farther than out of the door, out of everything, it never occurred to me we might not see each other again.

It would have come to the same if you'd taken us with you and forgotten us and gone off with your boat, that is how it feels, exactly. To which there is no reasonable answer. I kiss you as always, she writes, we both embrace you, we both do. It is you, I write, I am with, always. It also happens to be true, but no point saying that, no point, it seems.

I didn't answer, she writes, because your letter wasn't very agreeable. I wasn't glad to have it. One can be stung by such words, when one has written in good faith.

Days, I reflect, when only memories like dark birds blotting out the sky and drowning all prettier ones, memory of all the shaming and embarrassing things and only those, the disagreeable, the unkind, days and days of that, and nightmares. Or not shaming, not embarrassing, because hopeless.

Difficult dreams, she writes. When one begins to grasp, incredulous, what is in store for one.

It becomes quite impossible, to make you understand, there is a wall against which we smash our noses, she says, again and again, and my own eyes water, and yet you are annoyed with me for being hurt. I forget to write, I am not annoyed, so, by not writing that, I have dealt, without meaning to, another blow, and the wall rises to meet her, if you smash your nose, she writes, I am not aware of it, you hide it very well, there is no language, she says, there is no language I can reach you with, you are always impatient with watery eyes, you always were, that much, she writes, I do remember.

You write as though we're apart for ever and ever, I answer.

Your last letter has gone astray, says her next.

It is no doubt held up in the post. Letters with pages missing, or opened, reach me, but I make no comment.

You are well out of it, she says from the street, I shall presently hear you are prosperous. I answer, it is quite tricky, even without barbs, but I think you are not feeling well. I wish with all my heart I could alter it. She falls silent.

People shouldn't have to go about so raw, so naked, and then be ill and weak, on top of it.

I don't understand you, she writes, we don't understand you, you puzzle us, now we're on our own.

I telephone and speak to the doctor, our doctor, she suffers, he says, an infection, something ... the line is bad ... collapsing. I try to reach him a second time and there is only a long loud crackle ... very far away his growl.

Your recent letters didn't please us, she writes.

I should visit the doctor in person. I am homesick and long for her, and . . . there is prolonged interference, a crossed line, maybe, maybe not, the crackle drums for a while afterwards in my ears.

I don't think I can bear it, when you ring up, she says, out of the blue, you ring and I can't bear you to, the surprise. It is I, I think, I have brought all of it on her.

You were to ring yesterday, she says.

I can talk to Amor, and only to Amor, of the loneliness of living where the people are so strange. You don't explain; how, I've written, can I understand what the matter is if you don't tell me.

She writes, you forget to mention so many crucial details we don't get a full picture, you may know where you're going but you don't realise that we don't, unless you let us know your plans, your ideas for the future, the uncertainty is not good for us.

You can be sure you will be the first to hear. I don't say: I don't know myself, how am I to realise you want me to repeat, I don't know, I don't know.

One grows irrational, it is clear, when trapped and ill.

Boats are the last thing on one's poor mind, I must say, I have no energy for the boats you mean, no inclination, I talk with some pleasure to Amor. The name is an accident. Perhaps she had a sister called Venus, I don't know, a sister ship, who also sailed quietly up the river into the heart of the city.

So you talk to Amor.

One must be a little honest, she writes. I was imagining you had less time for embroidery. I have been myself foolish.

We are alone, she writes, and I am ill, we are cold, we are hungry.

Please do not fancy we suffer, she writes, we can look after ourselves, it is easier, indeed, than looking after you so well.

We need you, she writes, we miss you, we miss you dearly.

We live to see you again, she writes, we have hope, we hope it won't be long now, perhaps we shall be in a position to visit you, or you'll come, I don't want to go without seeing your face.

She stops abruptly. There will have been a power cut which she can't mention, and I think, I am away from all such nonsense. I am free to say in a letter, there is a power cut, I can't see to write, it is evening and already dark.

Then she writes, I think you must be ill, if you misunderstand so much of what I say, you aren't listening to me, you don't hear me. I try.

It's quite painful, she writes, for us.

To lovingly meant, heartfelt wishes for her birthday, she answers, thank you very much. It's kind of you to wish me happiness, she adds, in a tolerant voice, as though not hurting an idiot. In a squeaky hand, though.

She writes, so long together in the dark, and now.

The contents you sent we find useful and we are grateful for them, we join in saying we thank you and love you from afar.

It comes out in a little rush, she said to me once, then one knows it's fantasy, a little story, that it's not, she said, the truth, and, although one can't hear you do it, it's as if you've caught your breath, caught it up and then you go on.

Helpless to make you understand, she writes, deathly tired, I never thought you would leave us alone.

Day after day, such petty things, to struggle with, tiresome and silly.

I heard said of me, he has somehow mislaid his wife.

One has to sell oneself, I write, one becomes a cigarette or a bottle or a joint of meat, one smiles like a bar of dear chocolate and the path is smoothed perhaps, and one does that for ever and for everything, it is altogether harsher, in a sense, people don't meet you in the eye. Each is busy pushing in front of the other. Busy pushing in front and selling himself. It's more dignified to be a boat in the Ku'damm.

It is complicated, I tell her, one has to apply for it in the country in which one lands, and one has therefore to land where one has a desire to be ... but the desire is not to have felt forced to leave at all. It's complicated, otherwise. And ... I'd reckon, near impossible, yet one always is quaint enough to hope it won't be impossible.

Those in the most hopeless situations are the very last to lose hope, comes the smart reply.

More than water and forest there must be, you forget to tell us so much. You aren't telling, what there is, you don't waste words, for us.

I ache a little. It is, and is not, a paradise.

One doesn't need dollars or videos or Kent cigarettes or bottles of foreign drink or joints of meat but one does need money.

I can't reply that the shops overflow with food and clothes hang on racks into the horizon, the eyes squint, looking into the sun.

One is pumped full of impressions, almost to bursting, in the metro trains while one journeys one is told what one wants to buy and obliged ... I joke ... to long for it, perhaps that is good, it is quite cheerful.

Briefly my spirits rose. Then I learnt of your illness and the abyss for us.

I am, all the time, devouring the newspapers.

I don't blame you, she says, stay; to be frank, I like to think of your spirits. Rising.

It may be smuggled some day out to him by a kind soul and he will read it, if not burnt meanwhile. I am shaken, she wrote, to the bone, to feel the illness grave, stricken by that, and very alone, if we could but speak to him, speak properly, even in letters, on the telephone, he is cut off from us, I am shocked, I rub my eyes, I worry, it is hard to credit, and that if I go he won't be with us to provide, I fancy we are rather in for it, the soup, I so trust him, to hear me still. To hear, what I speak.

The fears are morbid, no doubt.

The state of forgetfulness and shaking accidents, the stumbling, and burning of fingers, spilling, bumping into objects, the cracking of the head, the state of that passed, and an uncanny silence.

But ... difficult dreams, she wrote.

He says that parcels exhaust him, and if I don't receive them are futile, but to know I've received the parcels and haven't mentioned them is the worst and the fingers tumble on the cardboard and string. He is busy with parcels.

We are disappointed in him.

Are you in pain, I asked her.

I understand, he was sure we could follow, and he was very taken aback to find it didn't happen as he'd envisaged, that my illness has wrecked any solution.

He tells me how to proceed but it seldom works as well as one plans.

I have the sensation of breathing always stale air, I breathe in and out and the available air smells of staleness, as though I have already breathed all the fresh air I was entitled to, and must make do with noxious, nasty air, that has been inside me once and is to go into me yet again, and again, for me there will be from now on this stale smell of my own air, of my own lungs, and no matter what I do, for ventilation, no matter where I am, indoors or out, I breathe the stale air, I take off all my clothes and put on washed, sweet clothes, so the stale reek comes not from my clothes, is not on my skin, it can only be my own stale air, no one else seems to notice, but I notice. I cannot tell him about the stale air, I wish I could tell him, I wish it, I do wish that, one needs to share such stupid notions, to help them to be less stupid, they craze a person, and they make one sad. He should have told us at once, as soon as he himself knew, not leave it, unable to grasp the thorn, it is understandable, it is human, but it is not decent.

Is it a stone, he asks, he can send medicine to dissolve stones.

And painful indifference, not interested in anything any more.

Then the moment, which was, one sees, for ever there, of sensing one is hurt, something has been cauterised and is numb, a door shuts and shuts again, a quick deadened for ever, so the hurt is to do with the loss of a wound, strange backwards sorrow. So, anxiety that the unhappiness should stay alive.

Better if he'd said it straight out, than leave me to realise slowly, always better to say things straight out, without pussy feet to make it seem more unkind later.

That if we can't come to him and are stuck he won't come back.

The post is painfully slow ... and she'd scratched this out, blacked it out. Painful post.

I am shaken, very shaken, she wrote, I said goodbye to him knowing I'd see him in two weeks, perhaps we shall never say goodbye again. He says, I realise you can't survive on your salary alone, the two of you.

I hope we see him soon, she wrote, I hope to join him soon, that we can is no mere dream, we have hope, we are buoyant.

But it is foolish to think of what wasn't true, one should remember what was, think not of lies and deceptions but of moments of happiness, sometimes moments of profound happiness. The hurt had life because one loved, let it have its little life, one can be tolerant, we are all fallible.

It does seem he had it all worked out, how we were to join him, it was innocent thoughtlessness, then, he meant all for the best. It seems he didn't have it worked out beforehand, he worked it out in a flash, when the opportunity fell in his lap. It seems he trusted us to understand. He was right to trust us. It seems he trusted us to keep wise heads, to be sensible, not to feel hurt.

The very words become stale, wounded, hurt, they too sit in stale air, breathed in and out so often, they reek.

I am stronger now, he should know but never will.

Hardship to do with foodstuffs, I cannot bear much more. He should know but won't.

On no one would I wish my plight.

I have the impression that it's convenient for him, not to know what is happening at home with us, it suits him to shut us out of his mind.

I do not believe he is so tortured, he is busy. I dreamt in the night I could speak to him, I knew it would all seem a nightmare, to be clean forgotten, bad while it lasts, and then over.

It must be that he is very unhappy, when he is unhappy and under strain he takes refuge in stories. One should perhaps not, it's naughty.

One has to be calm and listen, what he says often speaks, and is dear.

Oh come back, the thing is after all far more slippery at home.

So we can't help asking ourselves, for how long, over what period of time, was he thinking of it, his plan to go, was he still with us and in his head gone, already out of Lutânia, away from Prit, how many talks have we had cloaked in deception and dissembling, now he wants us to believe he didn't give it a moment's thought beforehand, when this would have been only human.

I don't want him to come back, for us. I cannot make myself be so selfish. But I am not sure I have the right to decide.

Often, so often, we spoke between ourselves of leaving, soon too old, we two.

Another train dream, another yet, am in a train, she wrote, no seat for me in the proper compartment, so have perched on a flap in the gap between the carriages, no stops, no stations, through the slatted door some scenery to look at, a different life, life itself, beauty; beauty, truth; as I trundled by, it was fluttering.

Not flickering, but fluttering.

One had to refuse fear, to live quietly perhaps, discreetly, but to keep a certain ... esprit. With such can one also be capable of stepping off a train to nowhere, when it stops.

Innocence, she wrote, is very precious.

How is one ever to know. Once there are stories. Only he knows, we can't know, what was true. Has he loved us, is it a story too, that is the question we ask ourselves, for it is forced upon us, however resolute we are in trying not to look it in the eye. He may know, we can't be sure. We can't quite rest easy.

We lie in bed ... she means, for warmth.

The words of despair, hope, anguish, happiness, they become absurd, without currency, called upon too often to have meaning, all the abstract words, all the words of the human spirit, it is better, she said, not to use them. The only words should be hunger, cold, health, ill health, money, money, clothes, food, dentist, doctor, work, sleep, dreamless sleep, house.

I am frozen. I am as if frozen, though quite warm, and she may be freezing. Helpless to act.

I speak, but you don't hear me, she writes. I worry about you.

Doesn't he understand, I'm worn out, I can't fight any more.

The loneliness, she writes, your sense of terrible isolation, it is due in part to your inability now to hear what is said to you, to relate to what other people are saying, whether in letters or by mouth, no wonder you feel as you do, no wonder, you are as if shut off from those who love you, and who are hurt.

Her beautiful handwriting isn't beautiful now, it's all awry, the once rounded letters broken and squashed, the ink not even blue any more, not serene.

I am so remote from you, she says in her letter, we are, from each other, I know these things wouldn't seem so enormous if I could talk to you, if you were there, if your face, in the shadow across the room, if I could put out a hand to you, if I could hug you.

More light.

It's hard to be two, but it's hard to be one, she wrote.

choosing spectacles

It is all a question of deceiving and teasing the eye, said the eye doctor, in order to obtain the truth, there is *no other way* of arriving at the truth, teasing and deceiving the eye and interpreting what the eye, or the brain, *thinks* it sees is the only way to the truth, so we eye doctors are party to a mystery, he said, hidden from ordinary folk, we set out to muddle the eye, or the brain, and the delusions the muddling causes, from those we know what further delusions, in the shape of spectacles, or lenses rather, to supply the eye with, and then again, he said, bobbing up and down, with a certain smug relish, only we eye doctors are aware of what absurdities are sitting on your nose, absurdities, given a place of honour, which render up to you, however, the truth, the true world, the world as seen by the rest of us, at least up to a point, taking into account local variations from person to person, in regard to colour, clarity, distance, though we pride ourselves on adjusting much of it for you, take astigmatism, or the world as seen by you before you needed spectacles, if you have slight astigmatism I have to correct it for you, never mind that you've seen like that for years and years, it will be in the nature of a treat, a treat for you, to see correctly for the first time, the first time in your life, which is why you have to grow used to them, to trust what you see, you may not oblige me not to correct your vision, I cannot permit my professional integrity to be

distorted, a treat for you to see through your new lenses, you
mustn't put up an idiotic resistance, you'll make it more
difficult for your own brain and your own eye if you do, only
stupid to make things more difficult, you have to, in a sense,
submit to this new truth, meekly, you have to accept my
word, that this is what you see, it is no use at all protesting
that you don't see what I make available for you to see, I am
giving you access to the real world, a true view of the world,
so it's unhelpful to protest that faces should be squatter or
trees taller, you had it wrong before, you see, dear sir, and
no, it isn't reasonable to imagine that after twenty minutes
of teasing and deceiving the eye isn't in a state to see
anything properly, are you not grateful to be enabled to read
as you did when you were ten, the smallest print, in a dark
room, under the blankets, come come, oh you've no idea
how amusing it is to confuse the eye, your eye, your brain, in
other words you, a pleasure for us eye doctors, if there is
something to correct, we'll correct it, shall we, if the muscles
of your eye are old and weary we'll supply a better focus, ha
ha, he said, you've no idea, either, how disturbed some folk
will be, you may have to persevere for months, better, wiser,
not to set up a psychological resistance, he said menacingly,
wiser, better, not, I assure you, you will make it harder for
yourself, there is no alternative, those are the lenses you
need to see with correctly, did I, he said archly, say
'interpret', well perhaps interpret isn't the right word, it's an
interpretation due to our skill, which is definitive, another
eye doctor will prescribe for you exactly the same lenses, he
said, mendacious, exactly the same truth, there are no
boundaries, no national borders, to it, you are not really at
liberty to disagree with me because the mystery of optics is,
so far as I know, denied to you, hidden, a pity, a pity for you,
it is great fun, a position, of course, one is placed in of trust,

one could cause havoc and distress, a position of integrity, so one can make the eye think, or the brain, one can bring about thought, create it, it is not something to be abused, I assure you, lightly, now take the script to be made up and choose, if not the lenses, the frames of your heart's desire, at the optician, you'll find him saner than me, I have to live in a world, my consulting room, in which to deceive is to be honest, the only honesty, where to *believe* the eye, what it thinks it sees, what it thinks, especially when presented with dots and stars and severed from its fellow, it sees, to *believe* it, would be to be fraudulent and corrupt, we need artifice, an interpretation, it is actually, he said, essential. A most vital element in our lives.

It makes me sad, that there is no life without spectacles, that there cannot be, one has to choose spectacles, between spectacles and spectacles, how one is to see, and sometimes it is forced upon one ...

Now I understand, says Camil, with a smile, a sightless smile, that for the joy, this leaving of my own country, I have to suffer, pay, I have to pay for it.

He is talking for too long. They are starting to fidget.

Well acquainted with the speaker, one sits, although *in* the audience, uncomfortably between it and him, with a horrible awareness ...

There are others on the platform who wish to exercise their lips. His listeners hunger to sympathise, but he is losing them. He is looking nervous and determined. He will lose them. They shift in their places and cough. It is already too late.

He trips up, stiffens, his eyes glaze, he plunges on, there is after all much he wants to tell them, a terrible much to be said, and he has been invited, he supposes, to say it, I sit in the audience and will him to wind up. It's been billed as a discussion, on the platform the others drink their water and stare at him expressionless, or with compassion. He may not be used, they think, to audiences. Yet he is. Different audiences, not so dry, not so impatient. All these broken people, broken-hearted or pining or simply broken, he says. In dreams still, thrashing in our sleep.

It doesn't, you see, become any easier, one grows accustomed only to that, there will be another place in which to find one's bearings, another language, another country, another town to be lost in, another world of feeling, always more difficulties, more anguish, until one thinks, soon, a heart attack, it is already too much, and one is weaker, and weaker, one is already too weak, and the nerves fray, and fray, and one has no strength for it, no more will, one is worn out, says Camil, exhausted, exhausted utterly, nothing left in one to give other people, nothing even for oneself.

The mind jangles: one feels safe, and cared for, above all safe, then something happens to make that feeling quite vanish, one is frightened, the fear of being ill, or that the nerves will be so jangled they break, no insurance to cover that, a limited insurance on the other, or simply frightened, in strange countries; at home, in what was one's own country, always the shadow of a disaster which could happen, and then did.

A man with a beard stands up, ten or eleven rows back, but you, he says, if I don't mistake, are a Jew, you can go to Israel.

And Camil answers, that is not for tonight.

All these stray people, isolated, not in great herds as after a war, he is saying. And presently in great herds, thinks the audience, mechanised herds, and no better, possibly worse. And for whom.

I think, in Berlin they choke and splutter pointedly on street corners and try not to cast reproachful looks. They are saying: put up the wall again, but fifteen metres higher. Or, soon they in the east will have their own supermarket shelves and can be locusts at home and it will all sort itself out. In Berlin they eye the shabby clothes with distaste, they say those from the east are all pasty-faced and have bad breath, and spots.

A few garlic plumes would be absorbed, not so easy to be welcoming to the great, tactless horde that heaves its passage along the Ku'damm and makes all the department stores unpleasant.

The white, unhealthy faces turn away, resentful, eyes don't meet any more. It seems they know it, they have an inkling of their plumes, they are sensitive, they are other. They are laughed at, behind their backs, it seems the German they speak is funny German.

One day the day will come when the Germans will have sorted themselves out, I think.

His fidgety audience is embarrassed by his loquaciousness, by his heart ... I know him so keenly.

A woman pulls a scent-bottle from her handbag and dampens her handkerchief, possibly she is next to a garlic breath, she presses it to her forehead.

It's supposed to be a discussion, or not, whispers a young chap in front of me. You asked me a question, Camil ploughs on, a good question, thank you very much for your question, I shall try to answer it.

So, you are fastened inside your own country, terrorised and bored and hungry and cold and you imagine that in the rest of the world people are happy and warm and fed and fed on the endless delights of television ...

It's true, shouts a person, I for one am happy and warm and fed, and when I was not I didn't complain, I set my hand to work and see where I am.

... fed on the endless delights of television and free enterprise, it never enters your head it might not be so delightful and desirable, that if you want to be warm and fed ...

Yet, I think, we never do learn.

... has to give in your ... I sit up smartly. They know, he says, *you*, dear listeners, know, not only how to *sell* your-selves, you know how to protect yourselves, and we don't, *not from each other*, we don't and we are not even aware of it, we are quite aghast to realise that some disagreeable eggs have hatched from our encounters. Our encounters, he repeats, waggling his cheeks with his fingers, as if not sure of the word's meaning.

And no defence against the demands made on us, no experience of these, because of a kind peculiar, different from the demands we have wearily gone along with all our lives.

The moderator intervenes: we had the idea we were to hear about there not here, we know here very well ourselves.

And we become more and more vulnerable, not less, goes on Camil as though he hasn't heard, not less, although the assumption, your assumption my dear listeners, is that we are, if not exactly assimilated or taking to it with gusto, wandering around in a haze of alienation, with a dulled mind, or heart. But one becomes a new invalid daily, fragile, like ill children when not fractious; hysterical, pathetic, one's own eyes seek anxiously for some gleam in one's own face, and find only strain and woundedness. A terrible sadness which won't go away.

He is saying words he had no intention of saying, he has departed from his text, it is plain. I see in my head the wild swimming of a duck.

It becomes a self-inflicted wound, he says.

Silence falls on the audience.

The moderator doesn't stir, the other guests on the platform are turned to stone, their faces flicker, they drop their lids and wait, once the moderator glances towards the door, they clamp their lips together, those on the platform, and Camil swats his microphone by mistake, no one knows what to do, and no one is interested.

Tired of getting used to places, Camil says, to beds and pillows and chaos, very tired, traumatised by each jerk.

They frown and wonder which hotel they've put him in.

Uncoagulated memories, says Camil, the constant disturbance of it.

So, smiling, with wide-open arms, we totter, babies, relieved, towards your system called capitalism, and with absolutely no idea of what we'll find there. Still folding paper in half for letters, kissing hands, ripe little targets for your amusement.

Camil lifts his hand, please, he says, let me speak, I beg you, one second, the moderator wilts in his chair, helpless.

He won't be asked to do it again, that moderator.

So we thought no one starved, no one slept on the pavement, that you didn't let that happen, we thought no one was left ill and alone and hungry, we have simply no idea, we come and it is grimmer than we could have imagined, it is hardly our fault, if we had no idea. He inclines his head graciously, I don't imply it is yours, he says to them.

We hoped you would give us your mind, on how the changes strike you, his neighbour on the platform says loudly, the changes.

The Bulgarian whispers and whispers with his interpreter, their heads together, and scowls, though smiling.

Beneath the table the crossed feet re-cross, the toe is stubbed again and again on the floor, or the itch on the ankle rubbed.

Besides, we have become a new kind of litter in the

world, Camil says. His calm look.

Your world in which misery is a badge, you who have plenty pin it on to feel happy and good, without it unnatural, so that if we tell you, any among you, a history, speak of exile and sorrow and wounds, you will say, it's like that for me too, I too am exiled, I too am desolate, you are not alone, you say to us, we all are, we are all alone, you will say. Lost, alienated, not at home *at home*, you claim to understand how we feel, because you feel it, you say, yourselves, profoundly, we on the other hand are, it seems, lucky, we have a focus, for it, for our sorrow, and you have none.

Now a sinister signal across the room, I am afraid they are going to cut his microphone, though perhaps it is linked to all the others and impossible.

Unnerved, he hesitates, he raises his voice anyway, as if it is his duty to carry on, technical problems are to be disregarded, like a true professional he soldiers on whilst a technician crawls on his belly over the cables.

Perhaps they're recording it.

Camil says: we have, it is obvious, this great incalculable sense of outrage, yet, although you grasp at least that, the things we choose to relate to illustrate it are to you faintly laughable.

It isn't that they don't want him to speak, but that others have been invited to speak too, faced with his enthusiasm for the invitation they are paralysed. But unwillingly.

The moderator glances at the redundant interpreter, the moderator's eyes shift around the room and fix themselves, strained, on Camil's lips.

The boy beside me makes me jump, he says: I may ask why you don't go back, or.

It is that mixture of awed respect for the figure of Camil and irritation, typically German.

They try to talk over him, he ignores it and they give in.

I reflect, no way on, and no going back. The obstinate words in the head.

The struggle, so terrible, he will say, does say to them, to get out, that the way back becomes blocked for ever.

Aha! And, someone says, what about us, we open our arms and you complain, you come in droves, an episode we shan't so readily recover from.

She is shooshed.

But to stay was too, says Camil, he hasn't heard, terrible; weak and ill where medicines are out of reach and private lives are meddled with and tormented in a succession of stupidities if one is lucky and worse if not.

He hasn't been invited, at certain expense, to talk of exile, it's out of date. It has reached the end of its shelf life, exile.

But brutality and silliness to be found the world over, you say. He directs a benign leer blindly at us. People can be vicious, one mustn't allow oneself to be so sensitive, do we really imagine no one is brutal or silly in Bonn or Paris or New York. He has never been to Bonn.

An intimate relationship with a country, rejected by it and rejecting it, one day estranged, another felled by the weight of longing.

An unstoppable longing.

I think, whatever has possessed him.

So, homesick for oneself! ... Their eyes quite cloud.

He gives them his heart, my dear Camil does, and they wriggle on their plastic chairs and sneak their cuffs back over their watch-faces. Some of them have the air of listening to a harangue in bad taste. His voice is grey with the effort of communicating, with his strange audience.

...yet another language, which is no language, yet another

country, which is no country ...

Watching, says Camil, the life drain slowly out of one, the senses retreat, and hope. Each disaster takes the place of the last, on and on.

And one wants to lie in one's own bed, with one's own bad dreams, with one's own sickness of heart, one's own illnesses and ailments, not, he says, to the audience, yours.

He looks at them, the hiatus surprises them.

Memory, he says, it is giving up the ghost, you know. So many things, day after day, that one forgets easily and is confused.

Either the feeling of being utterly useless or a labour so arduous the breath is driven from one.

Painful anxiety, painful physical manifestations of it.

And then, indifferent to a book, to music, to the new, no appetite, depressed.

Or off to America, perhaps, the new world, with high hopes, misguided, and one clings for a little while to one's misapprehensions though one steps over beggars in the street every day, the dying, those with the *sida*, until with shock one day one thinks, I shall end up there, on the pavement.

The pavement again.

One loses one's innocence twice, once in the east and again in the west, he says.

Stop, I think.

Other things will happen, other disasters, we shall be forgotten, stranded, well-meaning people will pat us, try to reason with us, point helpfully to our elbows, be cross with us, he says, history ...

His dignity, quite unassumed, is palpable. But they pity it.

... be cross with us. History is indomitable, and there will be more of it, fresh excitements, worse horrors, to lighten up the television screens. Washed up on the beach; and free, to return. In our former countries the great changes dreamed of are taking place, or have already, and there is no place left for us there, we are finished, and must live on, aware, it is really what exile means, not a temporary banishment but a rupture so total one can't catch one's breath.

History and climate, they have jolted on.

He thought out what he wanted to say in another climate. Perhaps Germany still has sensation in its amputated eastern leg, it may understand, because it's been there too ...

Camil has aged, since last I saw him. Ten years in fourteen months. Why, I say, why; one has to be polite, they deserve our politeness. Why, he says, isn't it true. I remain unrepentant, he says. But they were bored.

The terrible sickness, *losing so many years of our life to it*, says Camil, choking over his coffee, his cigarettes, desperate for relief ... we didn't ask for a cure, echoing his own words of yesterday evening.

The phenomenon of being hurt by society, I say, it's quite curious.

Camil blinks ironically at me, and coughs. One was hurt by that society, I say, and injured by this, all these from Dresden and Leipzig, with their forlorn look, too.

Wistful, never totally at home, and they are only the Germans, what of all the rest.

It is the spring after the autumn and the spring has started to bite.

Well I like the Rhineland, he says buoyantly, I didn't realise Köln was a pleasant sort of city, one could feel not bad.

Refugees from the east write messages into the void of the west and hang them on a washing line round a modern fountain in an old street: *we are two grown-ups one child one small baby we seek a room, you ask us to pay four times what we pay at home, we are despairing, we give up*; or, *you are afraid we shall take your jobs, and you are right, we are learning how to speak our mutual language in your mutant variant of it, watch out, we are very industrious and very hungry.* Cottoning on, says Camil, to elbows. In another hand, though, *a fool wrote it. You are inhuman here you don't know how horrible it is with you.*

The dirty washing in the morning sometimes is taken down. By the afternoon the line has been rigged again, I tell him. And passers-by stand, on their faces a blank intentness, as though they read in a dream, no compassion, for they look into themselves, into a forgotten memory. But the words don't go unregarded. They flutter.

It amuses him, as his audience did not.

Someone in this cheerful city must take pity on their need and have hung out the line for the messages, someone doesn't mind being taken to task for generosity and good will, he says.

No, the nearby café, I say, has noticed that it brings customers, an hour spent shuffling the feet at the fountain, soothed by the splash of its water, and then a nice strong coffee with cream and sugar and a vast slice of a delicious thing, black and white, and red where plums bulge or cherries.

Oh, shall we ... says Camil.

Bleating, says a spectator, pig wash, wish wash, they should make a go of it now they can at home or make up their minds here to be happy. *Capitalism is shocking!* A middle-aged woman smiles wanly, dabbing at her cheek with a silk scarf. *By stamping on people we are to gain society's approval!*

To be sure of a roof over one's head one has to crush one's fellows, we become strangers to each other, we are not at all used to crushing, we are scandalised, but apparently it is with you normal, and you in the west mock us, because we have yet to learn it.

The washing line answers: *with the best will in the world we can't take you all, and feed you and house you, and give you money to have in your pockets.*

The fountain's water is clean, do not dump your Trabants so near.

We have lost our novelty value, I say to him. He strolls on, with his child-like smile.

He feels ill, he has to sit down.

I think, and they had television.

But we, we arrived with heads full of poems and songs, to a world in which engineers and architects don't carry poetry in their heads, in which words of that kind are redundant.

Now the railway stations of Europe are awash with people lugging video machines, in their arms, or on trolleys several at a time, large cardboard boxes.

The high moral tone collapses, they ... we ... suddenly don't want literature, we seize on blockbusters and rubbish and pig books, a frenzy for pig books. In East Berlin, the bookshops fill with blockbusters and rubbish and pig books are for sale in the markets by the carrots and beetroot. Our bookshops too, I say aloud, will swell with that and Proust... Poor Proust.

I've never been in such a hotel, such a room as the one they've put me in, Camil says.

I show him the letter I had last week: she works half a day four times a week, she has this little job, it is she who earns the money for our food, the rent, our medicaments, the letter goes, from time to time I earn, it is hard but we aren't weeping, we are still thankful ... rejuvenated for a month or two and then abysmal ...

He fumbles with his food, eyes it with pleasure, beams absently at the waitress. Camil is almost an old man.

Coffee, he says dreamily, his expenses for the podium discussion in his pocket.

I am estranged from him. All one's old friends distant and dispersed, even when they sit beside one looking at the Rhine. We mind, if someone voices our secrets.

The guilt of being safe; physically, at least, safe!

The *bewilderment* of it, with full pockets, for the moment, when others are working as petrol-pump attendants and dustmen or have no means at all, no work, no resources, no hope.

Camil observes, one may seem to fall on one's feet, professionally, socially, that is, in society, but it's not so easy, one is marked by one's upbringing in a socialist country and *not in a bad way*, there is this paradox ...

And we move only from one kind of trivialisation of life to yet another.

Astonished to find there are lies here too! Camil says.

Is the human instinct right ... He is folding and opening his paper napkin very precisely. Right to fear chaos. Is it perhaps misguided in its fear. Is it a waste of energy. He lifts the back of his hand to his forehead.

It's funny, he says, what is a market economy if not chaos, it's order which came to grief.

Disaster, I think, has a new body now beneath its clothes, we are, each of us, free to bring it upon ourselves, whether or not of our own fault; no longer is it wrought by the state upon us.

It seems we, the flood, he says, from the east, are a danger, we have to be *repulsed* or *absorbed*. You are a little smut of chaos. How do you feel. His cough-cough.

Completely closed, I am thinking, so closed we never

confide in anyone, have no intimate friends, or only intimate friends we dare not trust.

But which is chaos, which order, he says, we shan't remember...

When, I say.

You're not listening, when we die. And what would one do without the other, it's a symbiotic relationship.

Closed behind this language which nobody speaks, too, I think.

Let's, says Camil, compare the goods, we have a pair of suitcases in Toulouse, the contents of those, each, and thirteen parcels of books, five to a parcel, my acquaintance Saïd has ... He plucks at his frown. Has besides clothes an old towel for his prayers. The person Saïd works for has infinitely more, two cars, a house in the city and a house in the hills, a private swimming pool, filled with water, wardrobes of coats out of fashion, shoes which give his wife corns, his goods seem inexhaustible ... untidy indeed. So who is chaos. We've never had such a roomy apartment and our neighbours see it down their noses...

A gleam.

Impatient with our childishness, I think.

Does that fine concoction, the Forêt Noire, whispers Camil, taste better eaten neatly, forkful by dark forkful.

I think: one can't go around tasting countries.

Why not splatter it all about, a child would, by choice, polite manners have no buds, it's your sense of order which munches through the mess, and why slice it to help it, why not an ice-cream scoop, a ladle, a shovel, all these implements can measure your money's worth.

I think: I, mysteriously all right, yet not, and my old friends, precarious in Rome or Paris or New York, or in Toulouse, somehow with their toe-holds more secure.

You would like to splatter it, I ask him, gazing at him with great amusement.

You have a stricken look, he says.

The rights of chaos, chaos too has rights.

I was seventeen . . . just as I saw her I woke. She was crumpled in a corner, she was going to stand up and smile, come towards me perhaps, perhaps embrace me, I waited in happy anticipation, at that moment some disaster, the disaster may have been the mere fact that I woke.

But I wasn't seventeen. I was older.

I think dreams don't know there's a plume of memory: for at the most twenty years can one bring back to mind what is said, what is seen lasts for longer, one is shedding the plume of memory all the time, and every once in a while a butcher comes and hacks slices of it away, or knuckles, he digs those out, like bullets from a wound, in general the plume drifts quietly off, and the tail of the thing will be gone for ever.

Why should a dream make a mistake about age.

She wanted me to go away, melt into the air, and with me the problem, I used to feel, her problem.

Such a liaison, in such a country, had been too complicated.

There was a woman clerk with her voice, so I dreamt up business at the post office. I wrote many letters, I sent off empty envelopes to myself, to my own address, our address, aroused suspicion.

I couldn't resist, and was forlorn the days the clerk with that voice, with Mirabel's voice, wasn't on duty, or I was bundled along the counter to another. Colder and colder, the quick dies in one.

In the stillness after the turmoil has subsided only a chill remains.

One may feel so sophisticated, one may behave so well, it is all so ironic, one is contained ... and then those moments when, carried away a little, one slips up. For happiness one pays, and those especially addicted to it pay dearly.

She has a queer expression, I said, your concierge. Mirabel said, it is those of us who have no queer expression you ought to beware of; and, they know all about you, all, don't worry. I looked at her. I hope not all. Better all. You are safer, she said, then. I stared, until she blinked.

I remember and remember how she spoke.

She was teasing me, in the dream.

Well, so somebody comes to play in Prit and so small and slender and young, she plays like an angel, her looks are truly ethereal, and you are entranced, she plays Telemann, and Bach, with her the instrument behaves as it behaves with no other, you dream of her, her music, for years, since you've introduced yourself, you've offered to show her Prit, you do show her the city, her and her aunt, the aunt who travels to all her engagements with her, you, and Lili too, you spend a day and another half day with her and you will never forget her, and then, said Mirabel, then, and at this point Lili glances at Mirabel yet doesn't smile, Mirabel smiles, then, she comes once again, the virtuoso performer, she is due, you engineer seats for us, all the three of us, you'd have moved heaven and earth, and the years have passed, the angel is older, seven small years older, she has a girth, stays, and clumpy shoes walk her on to the platform, her hair is crimped, her cheeks a little red and bloated, with jowls, and she plays, she plays the most wonderful music, she is at the top of her profession, and her reputation is well-earned, from her bow ethereal sounds, and you, you are miserable, because you no longer recognise her, even her hands aren't slender any more, she isn't pretty, you've been so excited and are now crestfallen, somebody pulls you out of the crowd afterwards, and draws you to her, she gives a crow of delight, she has a memory of you, you have a brief conversation in Russian, she has, you say, invited you to the rehearsal tomorrow, since you have a previous engagement you would have broken if you could have, if only you could have, and how you'd agonised about it, so ruefully, and then, you tell us, you won't bother to go to the rehearsal! Because she is old and fat! Is that why...

It is the nature of rapture perhaps.

Lili opened the sheet that had served as the programme for the previous night's concert, and we each read it afresh. It was as if every little movement had an unwholesome significance.

I had to go to the rehearsal, now I'd been invited, Mirabel said. I couldn't see why it was funny, she forbore to tell me it wasn't polite, I heard them both thinking it, and both knew it was useless to pursue it with me.

Mirabel drew concrete all day.

She draws, says the dream, what won't be seen and doesn't draw what will be.

There was no moon.

It was a bang which was the start of it, the kind of bang you think is the result of a street accident, as though a car has driven into the side of your building, in the street below, and you notice the glasses tremble on the table, they sing, and in the corner where the jars and saucepans in the kitchen are there's a rattle, a busy rattle and a cup slips, a few centimetres, stops, hesitates, slips more, falls, breaks, and it's as if a high wind slaps the building, a screech hangs in the air, a child wails, woken from nightmare, a siren is muffled and dies before it has begun, and ...

What is it, says Lili, in her soft voice.

An earth tremor, I reply.

The floor rocks, our feet swim in our stomachs, for five, six, seven seconds, eight, we half rise from our chairs, and sink, struggle upright, collide, we listen, to silence for one or two seconds and a strange, prolonged plop, even though it was pitch-dark we could see dust, a cloud of it, and our noses are full of it, Lili tried to slam the window shut and it was jammed, so we concentrated, the three of us, on the need to have it shut, we strained our ears. Only a squeak, and a few steps. How strongly it held, the instinct to stifle a crying.

We should go out, said Lili, into open space.

No, this is an old structure.

I'm frightened, said Mirabel.

The light paled slowly, into dusk.

After a long while, three-quarters of an hour, after we'd heard an engine, and surreptitious noises, and at last a siren, allowed to pour itself out over the roof-tops, after that Lili said, well, you must stay, you can't go home tonight, I'll make up a place for you to sleep here with us, you can't go home, and Mirabel looked at me with round eyes, and there was nothing we could do, to avert it.

I understood.

I was content to have her presence close to me.

Lili lit a candle. But a single flame, for the sake of safety.

I can't stay, said Mirabel, it isn't possible, it will be noticed. And so, I said. The anxiety she had no need to express. One knew too well. There is pain in understanding too well. The outside world wasn't to know Prit had suffered damage, or that some of its inhabitants had been buried, or that the number of dead was concealed, or that the metro flooded between Republica and Lenin, why, why, it was unsurprising, of course, yet bizarre. We saw with our own eyes what had collapsed. Don't cry, said Lili, and patted Mirabel.

Outside, there was a long hiss.

It's not proper, she murmurs, and glances towards our cubby-hole kitchen.

Lili trod loudly on a broken plate.

She can't hear you, I say.

Sh, she says, anguished.

... that I ... We both understand what isn't proper.

You are our visitor, I say.

To sleep at your place, her face says, after what has happened; what, surprise of all surprises, we've been up to.

Her face is transparent for the few moments Lili is busy with blankets, then it closes.

It can't be helped, you sleep with the husband, my face tells hers in its turn, and you accept the hospitality of the wife, of the couple, the wife who is in ignorance, I understand very well, but bizarre situations do arise and one has to make the best of them, and so live naturally.

Lili will discover us in unnatural silence.

But we were all tired after the excitement of the bad tremors.

In the dark, with our single candle, not knowing whether to run into the street or stay inside, not braced enough, we felt, for another shock, we were as people are with diarrhoea, ill-prepared and so unnerved into relaxing at the very minute it's unwise to.

Lili turned the knob.

The programme was over. No one was bold enough to announce to us an earthquake; a buzz, nothing else.

Lili tuned to Radio Free Europe, it's too soon perhaps,

she said. She switched on the television. The programme had finished hours ago. Tomorrow, said Mirabel, surely.

Lili went to the bathroom and changed into her primrose nightgown.

She had recovered her sense of the hostess, we won't cringe indoors, if we're indoors, my dream said she said, or clutter up the street, the firemen need clear passage.

She put Mirabel to bed, gracefully.

Mirabel had bags of energy, and she liked drawing concrete, the poor dear.

The sewers will have cracked, Mirabel said; we'll be contaminated, said Lili, in the dream.

Why should we go, I said, why. Because we are tired, said Lili. Without doubt we were exhausted. One lies awake, waiting for another.

We'll walk you home, Lili said.

The first workers were scudding by us, in an unearthly dawn.

I didn't sleep, said Mirabel, but not on account of being uncomfortable, I wasn't that at all, please don't imagine I was, she said to Lili.

We didn't sleep either, says Lili.

No trams ran.

They were digging for bodies, we kept our heads low, and suddenly Mirabel was crying, tears ran down her cheeks and because her head was bent hit the pavement where they made holes in the dust, like water when a fish has risen in it, we dared not comfort her, and Mirabel whispered, that was one of mine, I drew the concrete, the specifications, and I mouthed, don't be foolish; she said, truly.

It was no mystery, why the old buildings stayed up, and the brand-new fell.

And after the concierge of Mirabel's block had seen us,

and Mirabel disappeared inside, it stood, spotty and plain, after that we turned away and Lili's self-control left her, her composure went, and she too started to cry, we walked along, arm in arm, and she said, you don't deceive me, not for an instant, I know, she said, I know everything, and she cried, terribly, there in the street.

It didn't matter, our fellow citizens were positive she cried for the earthquake.

Only the uniformed clawed and dug.

By now a sky blue like a lake shone on to poor, damaged, beautiful Prit.

The electricity had returned at half past five.

Once, I'd said how lucky we were, we human beings, to have faces which could dissemble, which didn't tell the truth.

The tiny, dwarfed churches of the Christians rest intact, on the façades of the imperial buildings perhaps a lintel dipped, some stucco buckled, most of the city has stood up well, yet there is damage, there is, certainly, some.

People plod softly towards us; hover, blurry, to the rear of windows.

By mid-morning we all know where the epicentre was, a town in ruins, except for its few remaining old edifices, and explosions in its chemical works and escapes of substances, the substances vary in the telling, that's all.

Intact panes of glass, then, as we pass, splinter and we jump.

And a perpetual, odd silence, as though citizens have been removed wholesale; because it wouldn't be permitted, to those who have suffered, to give it a reality.

What kind of people were we, who feared to rescue the victims, did we know we too would be whisked away.

It's muttered that those affected worst have been taken

not to the clinic, where they'd have had the best chance of
being brought back to life, the specialist clinic in the city,
with its trauma unit, but kilometres from Prit, to some
remote and sleepy provincial town: why, one knew the
answer but faithfully asked the question.

The sewers had burst, in the suburbs; but the worst we
see is a water main.

Lili's militiamen loom up, and, on purpose, scatter the
three of us.

Then stiff-lips spoke to us.

What did he say, said Lili, in a quiver of panic, he said
good morning, and buck up, that was all, I reply, that was all,
she says, breathless; I promise you, I say.

I promise she'll never find out, I'd said.

I'm glad, said Mirabel.

Are you sure it was one of yours, says Lili, it doesn't
happen like that, and Mirabel says, you think I don't know
what concrete I've drawn, do they always let you in on the
secret, says Lili, of where it is for, no, not invariably, one can
guess, could you have guessed wrong, says Lili, to comfort
her, it's too absurd otherwise, that we should walk by,
perhaps it wasn't for Prit at all, perhaps you'll one day see it
erected in the provinces, yes, says Mirabel, in at least three
other cities it's erected, unless the earthquake reached the
north too.

You're serious, I say.

Of course I'm serious.

How do they fit, these buildings, in different zones and
with different neighbours, they tear down, she answers me,
what doesn't fit alongside, haven't you noticed.

I've noticed, Lili says unexpectedly.

I've noticed, says Lili, buildings which are only three-
quarters there, lopped off like branches of inconvenient trees.

I don't, I say, notice.

It's not supposed to be either wasteful or ...

We couldn't in our minds find an opposite of wasteful.

They in the west have computers for it, says Mirabel, for what, we say, for drawing concrete, technical draughtsmanship, whether the training is so long, so thorough, she says, I don't really know, I'd like to go for a course, in Paris or Moscow.

Are we the last country, says Lili, to do it by hand.

The time was passed, until the earthquake, with pleasant chat, it heralded nothing more than another week's toil.

I look at Mirabel and Mirabel follows Lili with her eyes whilst Lili brings cups and saucers, the cups with the thin gold line below the rim, our best china, and the dark blue glaze, very fine, inside, and the pot of coffee, and little sweet cakes, pastries, and makes room for it on the table with her left hand, balancing the tray with her right, and casting me a comical glance. I'm on a cloud, as usual. I start up, but she manages it on her own. Lili pours the coffee.

The new ideas had slithered delicate and pale out from the walls and sunned themselves; for it's during the enlightenment, so-called.

Once, Mirabel had come back with us, and Lili said she herself must first go for milk, we two should go on ahead, I feel Mirabel stiff beside me, and grave, we tread on, pass the sentinel, who's knitting, in silence, Lili may be four minutes or an hour or more, we stump up the stairs, it is dim, the daylight on the stairs, I open our door and stand aside, she takes off her coat, she says practically nothing, tacitly we've agreed something, I'm not sure what, Mirabel seats herself, her hands clasped, bolt upright, I smile at her, she smiles at me, her eyes say, keep a certain distance, I keep a certain distance, not here, her eyes say, don't even touch me, it's not proper, and we hold our breath, and quite soon Lili steps through the door, and doesn't notice the tense quiet, Mirabel starts to chatter, leaps up, so Lili says, do please sit, and Mirabel disobeys, smiling.

Once, I put out my hand and touch her breast by the door out, and she gasps, and places her own hand over it, on my hand; furtive moments.

I've been faithful, I said, always, almost.

Almost, asked Mirabel. I nodded. Yes, I said. She laughed.

I suppose we were accustomed to look people straight in the face, and read thoughts and feelings, those, at least, not hidden on purpose, in the west one has a sort of life on the telephone, although not on the telephone.

Trusted to be on our best behaviour. Does Lili sense something, said Mirabel.

No, I replied, no; and, I said, we are both fond of you and like to see you, you need not fear.

I hope you're happy, she said, with each other.

Yes we are happy, I said, I believe one could claim that.

When one feels already guilty, in an apartment with ears, possibly with ears, the truth sounds unduly loud, as though one had blurted out at a concert, say, a very private desire, or had sneezed without a handkerchief in the right pocket.

We used to laugh quite a lot together, being guarded doesn't stop one laughing, and Lili was guarded, she guarded for the two of us, and Mirabel, well, Mirabel looked after herself.

Mirabel was a member of the party, it was an essential, if she was to be promoted, she went through the motions, in any case.

She could be a cuckoo in the nest, said Lili, however much we like her, and I said, no! aghast. Lili drew her finger over an eyebrow, combed it, an eccentric gesture for a woman, and her hand shook, so she stopped abruptly, and her hand dropped.

I love Lili, I thought, I love her, I never want to be without her.

Word was passed with extra expedience, people felt for each other with relations and family dispersed peripherally.

The Academy of Art was ringed by troops.

Lili straightens her shoulders with a kind of gaiety, we round the triumphal arch, and so reach the street which led into the street where Mirabel lodged.

I can't thank you enough, says Mirabel.

I can imagine myself already in the office, you two should go back now, lucky to live so centrally, I wonder, the suburbs, she trailed off, the blocks in the satellite-suburbs.

You shouldn't dwell always on your job, Lili advised her kindly.

I could sense the warmth which came out of her body into her clothes, and steeled myself to part from it. I drew Lili's arm through mine, and disengaged it, for we both had to embrace Mirabel and say for the present, on this extraordinary morning, goodbye.

The sun began to blaze now.

I saw Lili's skin rise and sink, with each filling of air in the lungs, at the throat it fluttered but, as always, evenly.

We shan't be crushed, murmurs Mirabel.

Whole streets, whole quarters, looked exactly as they'd looked for years, it made the battered bits odder, ruffled, with that constant hiss of fire and water.

Lili is wonderful, to look at, said Mirabel, with apparent wistfulness, it struck me with great force when I met her first.

I haven't, for some while, I say, and Mirabel said,

shocked, but why, and I say, I'm not sure, I haven't, that's all, and Mirabel said, but that's quite shocking, and I said, I can't help it, and she said, but you must, you must help it, you can't withdraw from her, in such a fashion, what, she said, must she suppose, what must she feel, bereft, pronounced Mirabel, bereft. I gazed at her. I know, I said. But you love her, says Mirabel, yes, I said, I do, and Mirabel said, please try. I can't seem to, for the moment. You're too sensitive, she said. No, I said. It isn't so easy, to instigate, not even for a wife, she said, because she is bound to feel not desired, difficult to break the conundrum. I'm sure, I said. Please do see what you can do, next time you go to bed, Mirabel said, and I'll hope to hear good news. It's more normal. Tonight, that's the next time we go to bed. Of course, she said, strike while the iron's hot. But I saw she was disturbed. I understand, I say. Don't look at me so queerly, she said, I'm no monster, and I never want to stop, to lose you, I don't want us to be exposed.

The inclination, I say, has gone, I don't know why. I'm so weary, in the west.

Bring it back, summon it, she said.

We stroll in the Botanical Gardens.

You suit each other, she said. I wonder, does one cloak an immorality in a moral point of view, dispassionate, and deceive oneself, she said, and laughed.

But I'd sooner eat the peel than have no orange at all. Oranges, I protest, where are they; and she tweaks my sleeve.

I ached to embrace her, to hug her to me.

Her frock was a deep blue, like a workman's apron, yet soft and pretty. I forget, she said, exactly, I did, though, search Prit for weeks. Lili smiled, aware of how impossible it was to forget such buys, to find such cloth.

One was buoyant, insouciant, one had to be, it was to be free. Long depressions.

Well, are you still not, Mirabel asks, with a flutter of her fingers eloquent of anxiety. I think I must have flushed, or looked conscious. It's awful, she says, and I say, I can well imagine! She sighs.

How ironic.

She sat, hunched small, hands clasped; her eyes drifted over our candle-lit books, our pictures, as though she hadn't seen them dozens of times before, her eyes, awed, played with the contours of our things, and every so often left off, to dart a look towards me. I'd smile reassuringly, I was amused, to be able to read her mind.

Books acquired with such pains and energy.

Once, I suggested we go for a walk, and Lili said, you two go, I'd rather not, and Mirabel gave a tiny shake of the head and said, no no, we'll stay with you, she seemed not to want to leave Lili out of whatever pleasure was proposed, without a thought as to whether or not Lili wished for times to herself, perhaps Mirabel was in the right of it, though.

Mirabel's father had, after all, entrusted her to Lili. He would reappear from the provinces and wander Prit in a daze.

I shall leave, said Mirabel, in her obstinate voice. I shall leave.

It was before the amnesty, and so was final. Some manage it, she says.

The mothers and fathers of traitors should really die without seeing their children again.

I can't care, says Mirabel, I can't.

Lili frowned me down, crossed her legs, and the toe of one foot in the narrow shoe bent, flexed, towards the floor, and she smiled. Will you try one, Lili asked Mirabel, proffering the plate. Where did you find them, Mirabel said politely.

It isn't as though I was jealous, said Mirabel, or tried to prise you apart.

That isn't possible, I said.

Ah, said Mirabel, and you told me you were ready to fly, lucky I didn't misunderstand you, she says from the street.

Don't ring me, she said, it startles me, the telephone, I'm overwhelmed and my cleverness on the instrument deserts me, these hiccups and pauses are awkward, I shall never forget you, we'll never forget each other, I'll remember you always, please try not to bump into me or wander in my direction, actually I hope to leave, she said from the street, when the telephone rings I'm afraid it may be you, I'm nervous, I shan't forget you, you will always think of me, even when we're long and far apart, how is Lili, I miss her, said Mirabel.

You and I, we know everything, she said, about each other.

Lili cries, I said, in the night, her sleep isn't peaceful, I lie awake, and I see, and feel appalled.

Don't tell me, she said, please don't.

Papa has no suspicion, that I mean to leave, will you visit him, when I'm gone, is two hundred kilometres much to ask.

Of course, I said mechanically.

You think I'm not serious.

I'll stop, now, she said, we've spoken, I shan't ring you, it's too agonising, and in the street, to stand and people ...

She hung up.

She sounded close, but her voice was small and hurt and far away.

One can draw concrete anywhere, what an ideal profession, said Lili, concrete is wanted the world over.

Our courage, in my dream Lili said, isn't; ours isn't what's admired, in the west.

Mirabel at that time loved her father more than anyone in the world.

One had to do something utterly terrible.

Our Mirabel, said Lili.

Mirabel said, happiness is addictive. One sip and one is lost, I replied.

I can't tell him, she said, how can I, warn him, and how could it help, my father will know how it was, he'll write me letters I shan't be able to bear to read, he will hope, because he won't want to die without holding my hand again, I understand, that's the trouble, one understands all too well, better to be stupid and unfeeling, for oneself, that is, perhaps if he could make the journey to ... well he might reach Românìa, or Bratislava, Cluj or Bratislava, or Chernovtsy, or Lvov, and we'd meet, it isn't worth contemplating, actually, she said, I keep silence, then I go, then I regret, then he dies, then I die, some time later, I don't think, she said, of death, one imagines one is brought up brutalised, but it's more that one is made more tender, like meat, to be consumed all bloody and bruised.

Pulpy, she said, laughed, and cried.

I couldn't be more content with my profession, she said.

In my head I stroked her hair.

I have no desire to speak to her, Lili said, yet when she had to, she carried it off in style, only the turning of her cheek farther betrayed her, since also she had no desire to be embraced, however politely, by Mirabel, and when Mirabel came to embrace me, Lili looked away altogether.

We have news of her from her father; after the amnesty, which the need for *devises* provokes, she visits him.

How could she, said Lili.

I'm not so young, or so callous, says Mirabel, no doubt it'll be a struggle to start with, she says, without, she says, being over-blithe. I do suppose that, and I have strength for it.

I recoiled, gazing suddenly at the receiver, as though it had a sting or a forked tongue.

I remember, I must have shone in the Botanical Gardens, until the old folk on the seats narrowed their eyes at me, my light steps.

She comments: torn apart, as a couple of naughty children are torn apart, or mating animals … uncivilised.

So many occasions spent almost in silence, one fills one's own silence, and it's melancholy.

You know, she said, when you put your hand out and touched me, I was pleased and willing, she says, I've been continually.

I felt guilty and innocent all at the same time.

You're in my mind, she said.

I felt inflamed.

I felt an eruption of pure joy, tinged with sadness, a potent formula.

My fingers in her curls: not having curly hair myself, and Lili didn't, I'd never imagined how loose curls would feel to the touch. The back of the neck, and behind the ears.

I blurted out that I did love her, over the telephone, and Lili somehow understood or heard.

It burns itself out after a while, the passion of the pain, one is icy and limp.

Mirabel slept, where she lodged with an old woman, with the old woman and beyond her the old woman's nephew.

Fanciful Mirabel.

Once, we laughed ourselves into stitches all because Lili said the Americans didn't say hippopotamus, but hippo-potaimus, we each tried it out, to us it was a total tongue-twister, and we only had to try, to say hippo-pot*aim*us, one of us, for the others to double up with laughter, ever after, idiotic things set one off.

Hippop ... Lili would start.

It can't, says Mirabel, be, they can't ...

Hippopo-potamus.

Hippo-potaimus or hippo-potahmus, well, Americans ...

Tears ran down Mirabel's cheeks, we spluttered, hippopopopotamus, no too many syllables, hippopo ... Hippopotamus.

No one scrabbled in the rubble with bare hands, no one wrung them or wept.

I shall be happy, some day, to feel sure you're somewhere alive, said Mirabel. A deep bond, she said.

It always was impossible, she said, and also, how amazed we were.

So luminous and yet so grey, and an uncanny hush, a stealthy hush, when one has had an earthquake.

Once, I walked to think; now I walk to forget.

The bulldozer has been at work. It leaves behind it the fruit of its labour, heaps of blackened weed and wood, and of litter. It scrapes the beach raw, ready for summer.

I dream I swim out to a drowned rock at the mouth of a cove and fall asleep. I wake surprised my lungs haven't filled with water.

I stare down at the pebbles; stones that glisten, nervously licking their lips, I stare out at the sails in the distance and at the breeze in the pine-trees, I turn the weed over and over in my mind.

The train bustles by.

In the cove of that old dream, not pebbles. Small boulders, a beach full of boulders; one teeters across them, and they clack.

He sits in his little house across the lane and watches, what, he says, goes on. What does go on, I say cautiously. All and nothing. They are charming, he says, people.

Serge is, he tells me, an amateur, of what goes on.

The waves break white on a sharp protuberance.

The dream has adapted itself to France; now, I can look down on the island, and a sunbather is spread naked on its smooth rock surface. The pines on the cliff bend double.

How curious, that trees so stunted should seem so alive and vital.

The air smells sweet, radiant.

I didn't sleep, says Serge, I lie awake and have night-mares. His eyes are red. As though in rubbing them he's burst several small blood vessels.

One knows how much Béla paid for the villa, he remarks.

Its garden is a moon landscape, with lavender; pink stuff and blue on a trellis, and dark green leaves with deep orange-coloured flowers, creepers with vine-leaves; dragon-leafed monsters burst from lipped craters, magnificently spiked, with flower stalks the height of a tree, and prickly pear. I can name prickly pear.

Maybe it is the moon, and I am on it.

The clear light is reminiscent of Prit.

The resin wafts indoors, with scent of rosemary. The olives drop black, and stain the rock beneath, I hear their soft splat-splat. I follow the firmament through loose-locked shutters. The scratch-scratch-scratch is a clock, in the vil-lage, striking.

The sun creeps from the sea, and mounts upon the land, to the north farther by the day.

The church clock, yes, says Serge, quite correct; and that was the brother of the priest's mistress, he who paused then and said 'bonjour' through the cypress. He's modern, he has a mistress, the modern ones do, although he's old, but, never mind, il est brave. But I'm a communist, I vote for them, I can't imagine I won't always be loyal, he says.

Those are the nests of the caterpillar.

Béla should have paid for the helicopter, he didn't under-stand, didn't bother, there was a bit of paper from the Mairie, when the helicopter came the pilot flew across all our gardens, he didn't fly across Béla's. It's necessary. I'd ask Monsieur Bérenger to bring his gun, shoot the branch down, that nest is too high to saw off. Béla and Monsieur Bérenger, well, they're ... Serge sets his fingers ... with each other.

Since Béla bought the house I haven't asked it of Monsieur Bérenger.

Inside each nest are millions, millions of them, you don't believe me, ah well, tang pis, he says.

You watch out, they can be head-to-tail for two metres, on the terrace.

Serge runs his hand along the rail.

You mustn't let one touch you, you'll be quite ill, a dog or a cat can die, because they put their mouths to them and then swell and swell, football-heads, they suffocate in the gorge, or succumb to poison in the veins.

And you mustn't fall on a spike of the cactus either, he says.

Under the Judas-tree there's a snake when it's hotter, a snake likes to live under a Judas-tree, Judas-trees always have a snake, under them, if I see a snake, says Serge, I kill it, harmless or not a snake is better killed.

Go carefully, it may be quite chic by the sea but it isn't a town, he says.

The other employers don't ask Serge into the house. They sit him down in the kitchen with his coffee, or his bock, and drink theirs apart, in an armchair or on their terraces. Anikó is egalitarian. La France is very snob, says Serge. Béla and Anikó treat me like a faithful friend, not a servant.

So he has no objection when they desire him to drive at unconventional hours, for pleasure or to engagements.

He can't afford to have an objection, but he has none, in any case.

I suppose they are rich, he says, and a laugh cracks from him.

They threw furniture into the road, and ornaments, china, and pig books, all in Hungarian. The men, the refuse collectors, couldn't believe their luck, they held a small auction.

The refuse collectors made Serge a present of a pig book. It was a curio, he says, no one could read it, exactly.

The affair reverberates still. Maybe the pig books made an impact because, all in Hungarian, they were unsaleable.

Were they really pig books, I ask, not normal books. Were there pictures, how did you tell.

No pictures in them, that was the pity. Hungarians don't need pictures, he says, they manage without. It explains a lot about Hungarians. Otherwise, they're like us.

You, you are poor, he says. His voice softens, but his eye narrows. And Béla, he whispers. These are types with money.

I smile, I don't know what to say.

I am embarrassed.

I think, one forgets how potty people are. I feel close to these folk, with their childish stories.

Béla's car factory, he says, in Egypt, is big, isn't it. Prosperous.

I don't know. Yes.

They in the village talk, he says, they in the village suspect Béla of being an Arab in disguise. Why else would he cast out his Hungarian books, they ask themselves. Has anybody heard him speak Hungarian, our Hungarians often speak French, even to each other, whenever anybody is near enough to hear, and they name the child Georges.

It's comic, says Serge, what a village will say. Béla and Anikó, they are nice with me, and I love them.

The television has pulled up his van at your gate, Serge calls, to do your repair.

But he ignores Serge.

I think, there may be some truth in the theory of snob.

So we are treated to another spectacle. Only last year, the wall, Ceauşescu and Elena shot; and one waited for Lutânia to crumple in its turn.

I suppose we are all either victims or spectators. Serge erupts, as the sun rises, into the room through the door to the terrace. It is the second day of the war.

The operation *Tempête du désert* has been unleashed.

Politeness forces me to turn down the volume, offer him coffee and listen to him.

But I must be making covert glances at the screen, it's my first full summary, or was, of the news, I've been in the night to bed and now Serge pants, is in a state of fluster.

Because he frowns at the picture, as though unable to focus and then at me, puzzled.

I disturb you, he says.

I wrench my eyes away.

The doctors want three thousand for Patrick, he must bring them three thousand, or they won't do the operation.

There was no money yesterday, the banks ran out, he says, the Post too, because of the panic. I haven't ten francs, I haven't, he says, the cash with which to buy bread.

He has no money to buy bread so I reply, let me help you out, I haven't much cash myself but you could have half, I say, of what I do have.

He blinks, and smiles, tremulously.

No no, but I'll come to you, if I need to, he says, if I'm desperate.

The doctors insist. They're brutal.

Why doesn't the insurance cover it. Why doesn't the state take charge, I say, of it.

I don't know, I don't understand, but it doesn't, he says, and he shrugs.

Patrick's condition should, Serge explains to me, have

been corrected in infancy, and no one told them. Hardly fair.

But what is it, I ask.

He says, it's a twisted penis.

I think of the large penis, thoroughly twisted, one stepped past on the stairs at the Akademie der Künste in West
Berlin.

It needs attention, or it'll make problems for him later on,
they say.

The physiotherapist comes, he says, it isn't enough. She
comes, and for that one doesn't pay.

But what, I think, does she do.

I've been to all the employers, and they all refuse. They
would, he says, with a degree of contempt.

Will the bank lend you the sum, I ask. Couldn't you
speak to someone.

It isn't a bank, it's the Post, and far, in Fréjus, one can't
talk to the Post. I own no house to stake, in any case; my
house isn't mine, my land isn't mine. It belongs to somebody, and he won't help. His voice catches.

The doctors bully me, he says, and confuse me. I have to
find it before Monday.

I don't dare dream, he says, Béla would come to the
rescue.

Why Fréjus, I say.

It so happens.

I was over in Fréjus before the mother of Patrick went, he
adds, glumly.

The supermarket shelves are being quite denuded, he
says, by the panic. At Champion they couldn't work hard
enough to re-fill them, and soon the stocks will be
exhausted. I've kept Patrick from school. It's risky for the
children to travel by train. Toulon isn't safe. There was a
bomb at the station, a big police alert, did you hear, an

abandoned parcel, a hoax, but next time it could be a real bomb. They say, there are too many Arabs. We have lots of them, you know, in this part.

You should buy yourself some rations, he says. He knows I'm impractical.

It was to the outskirts of Toulon, in April, nineteen eighty-seven, that his wife took off, almost four years ago.

She hasn't been seen since. One has these implacable feelings, he says. I've no sense of ill-use, she upped and went and left me Patrick, for which profound thanks. I do my best. One must!

If Patrick and she meet, it may be possible they do, I have no notion of it.

And you, are you married.

I make a gesture of my disinclination to discuss that.

Mm mm, you too, he says. So your wife too. It's unfortunate. I don't mope. Do you. I have one last employer to try, I must go, I regret it.

He stares intently at the screen. It'll be long, painful, the casualties will be high, they warn us, he says; let us hope for none in France itself.

I have TF1 on, there is Michèle Cotta, exhausted and pale.

I say, I've been to bed briefly.

You look at television but I, he says, watch the world.

Ah, I assure you it doesn't come from me, he says, it must be the fault of the mother.

I tell him I had no such idea in my head, but he wants to reassure me; there's never been any twistedness in my family, he says.

He never knew his father, I remember, and his mother died young.

I think, does it matter.

Fancy! he says. Gas masks!

Two Scud in the night, I say. Twelve are lightly wounded. Tel Aviv and Haifa were touched.

Yes, he says. I wouldn't let Patrick take the train to Toulon. I told you, didn't I.

I peer from the terrace. You have a caller, I say.

The femme de ménage, he says, as though he's forgotten her name; the little countess.

The Revolution, it made ordinary fellows of them; for generations now, normal. The taxi, he's another, an aristocrat.

She washes my floor, he says.

I switch between TF1, Antenne 2, and La Cinq.

We are rallying, someone familiar states, all our forces, to bring the latest news to you, the analysis, the images.

The camera rakes the supermarket shelves of Nice. It is Nice which is the seat of the panic. We are asked not to follow the bad example; and not to hoard.

Serge probably, I think, has a cache of petrol for his car.

The télé doesn't mention the hottest fear: Gueddafi, if Saddam Hussein can hit Israel with his, can dispatch missiles to the Côte d'Azur, we are in his range, the distance can be measured on the map.

The neighbour says, well, we have a cocktail from Nice to Marseille and beyond, in Marseille in particular, of the pieds-noirs, of the Maghrébins, of the FN; although, he says, we are in the village without Arabs, they haven't penetrated so far.

He is a Parisian.

The week-end passes: anguished suspense. Serge is kept busy. They defile on to the streets of Algiers and Tunis, sous le choc. Then Dharan and Riyad are reached by the Scud.

The long, elegant face and grave eyes of Ruth Elkrief,

roped in from duties, it seems, less prominent, to read news summaries, bursts upon the male population of France. I too wait for Ruth Elkrief to smile at me. I catch myself smiling at her in return. I like her blouses.

France is uneasy, though Marseille is calm.

Serge rings me, after, he says, tossing all night. It is Tuesday, the twenty-second. It's you, he says. You're not asleep.

If you come to the window, you'll see me, he says.

I look across to his house. He's hung the caged bird out, though it's still only half past seven. I wave, and, there you are, I say, with the receiver to your ear.

It's serious, he says. I want to ask you, have you by any chance spoken to Béla and Anikó.

Briefly.

Did you mention my trouble.

I did sketch it, I felt you wouldn't mind.

He's silent. Seen across our two hedges and through the two windows his head keels.

So Béla ...

He didn't really comment, I say.

I hear a weird kind of groan, a sob.

I say, you're in low spirits, do you want to come for a chat, to drink some coffee.

I will, he says.

Lachrymose, he blocks me from the television. I'm at my wits' end, I shall go to prison. Look, my hand is trembling. You are kind, you.

I switch off altogether.

Did Patrick go to the hospital.

He didn't go. They put it off until today. One interrupts you.

I suppose, after four years and a month, I am still avid for it, I say. Does Patrick go to the clinic on his own.

A copain is with him, says Serge, abstractedly.

I wrote a cheque! he says.

It burns in the pocket of Patrick's trousers, without it the hospital won't act.

I, he says, have no money. I paid one thousand five hundred francs for the tests alone, my account is empty. I told Patrick to hand the cheque to the doctors. I had to, had to. But now, he says, I have to acquire three thousand for my account, or I shall go to prison. The cheque will arrive back at the Post. I'm quite afraid.

Prison! I say, what, straightaway.

One goes for far less, a fellow in the paper, he offered a note at the cashier in Champion, he'd no idea it was false, but they collared him. You go to prison and argue later.

You understand, he says, you do, because you are poor, how one despairs.

Was the case so urgent, I say.

The doctor told me, it can't wait. One can well imagine, he says.

He is casting around, frantically, for extra employment.

Yesterday I even went to be a night janitor at a small factory, almost an hour away. But I didn't succeed, he says.

He looks at his hands. I never stop, Serge says. I started at fourteen, the age of my son. Is Béla industrious, do you suppose.

Very, I say.

He puts his glasses on for reading and pores over a lot of bundles in the garden.

Mmm, I say.

Like you.

Mmm.

What does one set up a car factory from Hungary in

Egypt with.

With flair, I say, no doubt.

Serge nods, in complicity. Neither he nor I, we are not in possession of flair.

I don't really know. Perhaps there's a market. I do quite well in a deckchair, I say humbly.

It shakes, I can't control it, he says.

He spreads the fingers.

One doesn't feel it in the bones, one doesn't, when one has plenty. One doesn't suffer because one can't keep a child in health. One doesn't labour one's guts out and still scrape by from week to week.

I could sit, I think, and stare at him and pretend not to understand.

If I hadn't felt guilty about my being an intellectual, I might not have melted.

I can let you have a thousand, I say. His face falls. Does that help.

It helps, he said.

I have a hollow pit in my stomach. I think, I can't afford to lose a thousand francs. I'd meant, *to buy bread*; not half of all I possess. He must realise, surely.

I pass him two five-hundred franc notes.

You'll have it back, he says, it's a loan.

When you can.

I shall try to dwell no more on it, but it wasn't my affair, I think. It is Béla whose employee he is, Béla who persuades him to drive at all hours to Les Baux or Grasse or St-Paul-de-Vence, to whose whims Serge panders.

I begin to feel impatient. Serge has run to me in place of Béla.

I ring Egypt.

Look, I say, look, it's Serge, he's in distress, obviously I was supposed to ask you, I didn't when we last spoke, he was practically weeping, he's written a cheque, Patrick will have given it to the doctors, and it'll bounce. No one else, none of the other employers, will listen.

Serge has some family in the village.

He says not.

Well, some family elsewhere.

No he says. He was with me a whole hour. I thought he was going to break down entirely.

Has he no assets to dispose of, why did he buy that baby tractor for his half-hectare.

To pay for until the year dot. I say, I gather it isn't his half-hectare, he's the tenant.

Yes, true.

He's in a state.

I should think we're well out of it, says Béla; sounding, in Egypt, far off.

I am chilled; I say no more.

Is all, he says, in order there. Is the weather pleasant.

I avoid Serge.

Ruth Elkrief will find you towards midnight, says Poivre d'Arvor.

I've noticed the weariness in her face, in her low voice.

You are numerous, those of you who admire her, you've telephoned and written in, many of you, vous êtes très nombreux, to tell us, the rédaction.

Perhaps, I think, she has small children and puts them to bed, then comes to us, to smile at me.

One does everything for the children, Serge says, then one dies, and they come in colours to the funeral.

What has happened, I ask him, has Patrick been operated on.

He nods.

And the cheque.

Ça va!

But he doesn't elaborate. I forbear to interrogate. It's not my affair.

Patrick is at home, he'll be across to chat to you, he'll split you some wood for your fire. He's cool, le gosse. He dealt with the doctors, he had to be a bit adult. I couldn't accompany him, and the school-chum is an idiot.

Tell me, did you speak to Anikó, did you speak to her, to Anikó, of my difficulty. I wonder only.

I shake my head. To Béla.

I look at him. But Serge studies the floor, uncommunicative.

With Béla I have, I say, had two words since. To do with the invoice for the domestic fuel.

Because it was so far as I know no-go I dissemble.

How is the hunt for work.

The hunt is suspended.

I'm bewildered, yet don't pursue it.

Béla speaks seven languages, the neighbour says so, says Serge.

He speculates on his fingers, French and English, Arabic and Hungarian, Arabic, no, Russian, Italian, six, and Yiddish.

Why Yiddish.

Doesn't he speak Yiddish. I thought he spoke Yiddish. Oh I quite assumed he spoke Yiddish.

No, why should he, I say. He isn't a Jew.

Mother Arab, our neighbour says.

Hungarian.

That's what I told him.

I say, the neighbour is bizarre; but, I can't help it, I do like him. He's good-natured towards me.

Serge says, fine for you, you're educated, with me he can

be snob; this I overlook, though, he adds.

I speak only French, but Patrick, he speaks English and they learn Provençal songs at school. His English is superb, the prof has informed me. I say, speak it for your father. He shuts his gob, and pfft. I'll tell him to come and talk in it with you.

My English is poor, I say.

Don't you speak English.

Really, not at all.

They, next door, they spend a fortune on surgelé. She cooks entirely from it.

I believe the French surgelés are the best in the world.

Of course, I think, it matters, who is rich and who is poor.

You can hear Patrick, and he'll be satisfied.

It may be that Serge is happy to hide from me.

I go stiff to bed, see the lamplight on the armoured leaves, but his light is out; left to himself, he'll be asleep by nine and dressed before dawn; when Béla is overseas and no service is required. Patrick is invisible on the other side; he won't be torn, says Serge, from the shows, late dodo for him.

The fortnight goes by.

Béla telephones quite often.

I sit by the télé, in a trance.

I chat with Anikó.

It isn't mentioned.

She writes, and I answer.

Minutes, to walk; hours, to view the actualités; some minor, too minor, intellectual toil.

I think, why did Serge have to go and keep us all in the dark, perhaps he was confused.

For Anikó, after the battle of Khafji, has said to me, you know, our cheque didn't bounce, when I read your letter I rang Serge.

You sent him money!

Béla told me what you'd told him, and I felt we should help Serge.

She said, it concerns me, that Serge should be in a tangle; but he is, I can't find a word for it, she said, pure; we depend on him, he's always amiable, night or day he never grumbles at us. We treasure him. I shouldn't like it if I needed medical treatment and wasn't able to pay for it.

I said nothing and thought of my teeth.

Serge is honest, said Anikó.

How tender-hearted, sweet of her.

Yes, says Serge, in fact Anikó did ring me, you'd made her suppose I'd had trouble with their cheque.

Slow to respond I say, I had no idea she'd sent you a cheque.

Anikó is kind. He stabs the corner of his eye. You must have told her of my worry. It's thanks to you. So I thank you.

They sent you three thousand francs.

Yes!

You had need of three thousand, and you'd had one thousand from me. Between us we have provided four.

It's all gone.

Gone.

Yes, the doctors have demanded more, it's all gone.

I don't understand, I say warily.

They had to have more analyses. I don't, he says, myself, get it.

But it was an anatomical condition.

Of course.

I wish I could explain it to you, he says, and he sighs. Patrick may have picked up more.

I suppose, I say, you should return the first thousand, when you have it, to Anikó. Wouldn't . . . wouldn't that be right.

He hunches his shoulders.

It's incomprehensible, he says, why she didn't mention it to you.

Anikó is discreet.

I think, the four thousand francs fell into his lap.

To her I say, are we corrupting Serge, do you imagine.

I think, what possible business have I to take a moral tone with him.

I didn't confess, I say to her, I'd let Serge have some money myself, because really there was no point, Béla killed the subject dead.

Serge roars in his garden. I listen, go indoors, shut the window.

I shall never get to the bottom of this dreary histoire.

I now wonder, have I fallen ill to some disease, or should I rejoice, to be assimilated, and so soon, in a matter of three-four years.

If, I think, in a dark mood, I hadn't been painfully stuck to the télé I might not have offered half of my money. I don't believe Serge had it planned, he was too distracted to notice that he'd laid a snare for me with his no-money and no-money-for-bread, for three days he hadn't slept, he didn't realise. But he did force me to honour my word, he came to me; was it cunning or naivety; and when he found four thousand francs in his lap, what was that.

I pay, I pay Béla, I remarked, a contribution to the costs.

I was incapable, it seemed, of splitting wood. You bang down, observed Serge, on a place that bounces, there are not many which bounce and you have to go and choose one of those. The axe isn't mine, I explained, I don't want to damage it on rock. Take a fat log, Serge said, put it on stone, and split the other on top of it.

So I was branded an intellectual; had what passes for knowledge; I had to be infinitely richer than he; only those who work with their hands can be called truly poor.

It was a mistake on my part, to be frank with him, tell him I had a sum in my pocket. I had, had I, a lump sum, an untold luxury. That it was the meagre ration for the months ahead was unreal. For he said, I never have such a sum, I have to earn it, look, see it under my finger-nails, week by week, hour by hour, never enough, always gone. No intellectual in my country was a stranger to manual labour, but it had to be, I said, labour of a kind totally unskilled; then I laughed. He was puzzled and I didn't elaborate; even so I felt the justice of his argument; he narrowed his eyes and said I'd won a better life all the same, I was better off than he; absurd to measure oneself against a man who has no permanent right to live; however, I saw the force of it; I was on his side, with the poor and insecure; and felt a wave of brotherly compassion.

So, now on my conscience, that Anikó has been stunned, by Serge, whom she treasured. I feel at fault. I may, when Serge first confided in me, I may have uttered the fatal words, 'does Béla know'; what possessed me. I was the one who could least afford it. Serge had baffled me by commenting on my shoe-laces, the funny way, he said, I tied them; for no reason I was embarrassed; he showed a shrewd smile, of triumph; what is life if one isn't observant, he asked, rather empty, I imagine: en Loutanie, I'd have lent or handed Serge the money without hesitation, so why should I, in the west, ponder whether it was wise or not, or foolish, kind; unkind, by that one means apparently one should fend for oneself, be self-reliant. Serge has a magnétoscope, a roof, a car, pairs of shoes, it was ironic, he has the little countess, I thought. You, you have no children, said Serge, once one has a child not a day passes without some care, you are lucky, you may enjoy your freedom, why not; he rolled up his sleeves. Shuttered houses in the winter are many, people who arrive for two-week orgies, and go back to Paris, wait, Serge said, until the cinéaste comes, music and screams until three or four in the morning; he's not too snob to forget Serge, said Serge, he drops in, asks if I object to a party, it may keep me awake, a decent type; who when Patrick reaches sixteen will invite him to an orgy; a promise. Dismay. The reflection, that I'd wasted my money; had I but known; it made me rage for a second; appalled I should see myself in loco parentis. Serge said, good friends; feudal, said Anikó; heaven help him, I thought. Serge said, some day the Côte d'Azur would have an earthquake, the newer houses would fall; the villas of the rich; only in Monaco was one regulated, rich and poor alike, and all buildings built to withstand it. In Rabat, five hundred thousand manifested in the streets. The English troops in the front line had, we learnt, been vaccinated against the plague. The neighbour said, slaughtering ewes, pfft, like that, with a knife, God on their lips, why should we give them social assistance if they won't live as we do, quietly, and clean, they live in squalor; to the Arab, cleanliness is of great importance, Serge said he said to the neighbour. Serge said, that's what I said, and he said, to us; no, to them. You, have you experience of Arabs, asked Serge; a little, I said, in fact, yes. Boum-boum music all night, he said the neighbour said, they shouldn't bring their habits to France with them but absorb ours, of courtesy, of honesty, conduct themselves; and the Israélites, well, they slaughter with the knife too. I don't agree with the FN, but they, they of the FN, have a point; the Maghrébins pour into France but we can't go and make the old places, l'Algérie, profitable, the neighbour said, no, we had to feel the tail between our legs; but Serge had himself, he said, bland, no feeling against Arabs, although many did have it; Arabs in France are mostly poor, and he knew what it was to be that; and you, you do, he said.

I'm lonely so I listen, I think.

You'll have to lose your innocence, had said Béla. Why haven't you.

To Camil, I send a letter, but who, I say, who is innocent, and what does it, in the west, mean; one would imagine we had cynicism, if that's what's demanded, in our veins, from birth, how else would we have managed daily.

Is innocence different, in the west.

Saddam . . . Hussein . . . à la . . . maison, sing the French children.

They arrive, Serge says, decapitated, their heads have dragged on the road because they've had no more strength to hang on, stowed underneath, or have suffocated, with two dinars in the pocket, and no identity papers; starved and incarcerated, they still arrive.

Transfixed in a floodlight on a border bridge, beside a railway, illegal, unwanted. To catch them, a small victory.

The Abbé Pierre tells us this isn't it, the invasion, that's for the future, why should we imagine they'll stay where they are, in the countries of the Maghreb, in Africa.

Don't say that, says the interviewer, Anne Sinclair, you'll frighten people.

Yes, I dare say the only truly moral position is to stand back and let oneself, says a letter from Toulouse, be trampled underfoot, behind the shore. But people fight like termites, are weakened accordingly, have an empty victory, have won.

Then in the business of push and be-pushed one ought not to push yet pushed one should yield.

I think, chaos, les nomades, les Arabes, les Maghrébins, les noirs, les Juifs, les marginalisés, les exclus, Saddam Hussein, Gueddafi, les immigrés, the list is rich.

How can we say, says Abbé Pierre, you are de trop, you and you and you.

There would be the distasteful spectacle of the thousands and their being repulsed from the honey-pot, Camil scrawls, soldiers lining the beach, were the hordes to decide with one heartbeat to fling themselves on France.

Chaos fights for both sides. Chaos is a mercenary, I think.

With his drowned eyes, he scrawls to me, all these new rights, the right to know, the right to develop.

He was silenced by their calling him to the telephone, urgent, pardon for the urgency, he looked startled, somebody could have been taken to hospital, run over, in Toulouse, he collected himself together, apologised, to the audience, to those on the podium, and trod with sombre steps away to listen to his bad news. The excuse was thin. The hotel had felt there was a forced passage into his room, which had meanwhile proved false, he could resume his place on the podium if he cared to disturb them all again, he elected to slip in to sit at the rear. The ruse was so transparent and gauche it humiliated him, though he smiled, my Camil.

In Irak, in the desert, the allies camp, and fold their arms, before Basra.

I'll drive you to the station, Serge says, are you packed and ready, one good turn deserves another. I suppose it's like walking the plank, he adds, unexpectedly.

You'll have your money! Of course. You're off, and you must have it. Thank you.

Shall I pocket mine, I wonder, quick. I make an inward grimace.

You head where.

I head north-east; to my sorrow.

Serge gazes inland, to the mountain. Theirs I may set against my hours for them, Anikó told me so, pay it back when you can, she said. She knows some day, she said, she will have it.

I look at him. I think, the poor pay a terrible price, to the rich, for the kindness of the rich.

Bon courage-a, he says.

I'd rather live in France.

It's evening. I go for a last stroll by the sea.

Wearily I walk along the road to the coastal path. Smart gardens with black PVC water pipes line the cliff. My good shoes are dusted white, the stones scratch them. I hear a pop-pop in the distance, true, but am unalarmed. I drop, most probably, a piece of paper. My feet make no noise. I skirt an odorous hedge, rampart of clipped cypress. I come to a gap. I glance through it. A man has his gun pointed at me. I'm shooting the caterpillar, he explains. The barrel is lowered. He rocks with guilty laughter, his moustache twitches, he waves at the nest above our heads.

I am overwhelmed by a feeling of shame.

One could look straight out to sea, somewhere there will be the opposite shore, l'Algérie, la Tunisie; somewhere, still on the opposite shore, Tel Aviv and Jaffa; though, for me, *a long while ago now....*

I see her as a kind of prickly pear, not unattractive, with those little flowers perched on the rim.

The chicken manure in her village, it's being turned, the fowl dung, they do it to dry it, then it smells, a strong stink rises and overpowers the sweet air. But it isn't bad, it's part of life, celestial in comparison, if one remembers exhaust fumes. Especially ours, 'your exhaust fumes' she says, our Trabi and suchlike fumes. They have this abrasive manner, of course. It will be sold in bags, light, friable, matured. Most, most effective.

It was all drunk in, her chicken manure, the uncastrated cats and wandering dogs, the sheep with scrapie, mulberry-trees and the old road along the wadi, her snakes, she drank it, her tortoises met in the forest, her bulbuls and dinosaurs, hoopoes and storks.

It's wet manure she's used to.

The moshav has washed its hands of its unpruned orchards, let them go for no rent; because, too close to Jerusalem, they'll be swallowed up; one spots the surveyors already at work. But until swallowed better producing. Better to have plums, for prunes.

It's nature, or is it, when it burgeons, her notions are different, all these puppies and kittens, should one let nature slink around with ribs sticking out, with festering sores, let it multiply itself where, in unnatural conditions, civilisation, there work no natural restraints, checks. Should one shrug one's shoulders. Cheerful.

She doesn't know, one doesn't, not for sure. One can't ask the cat and she suspects the cat mightn't know either.

One can't be.

Only that one lives in a world in which many are too sure, of something. I'm probably one of them.

I muse: that is *her* luxury.

You're in bed, you're chilled, you've eaten poorly, two hours ago you burnt your diary; two months ago you were pilloried in a rag; you have to dare to open your mouth; and you're bored; worn out by lies, the grotesque lies, by the grind: you may laugh and smile, but you do know why, how your condition has come to be so, who is responsible.

One does, does one! Ho. Her blank face. Is she so naive.

It is I who am quaint. If I speak of art, I am not to speak of art, I am not to talk of literature.

Her curling lips are hard to interpret.

Lady novelists are genteel, with buns. It was a witticism.

Buns.

I think, there may be a problem of language.

I may call her a woman writer.

She turns her hand, she is a professional, a Mozart, turning her hand, for the money.

It would positively break her heart, to have to eat the books she'd rather read, and films and all the music she'd rather see and buy and listen to, not to have a shekel left over, for the spirits, for wider horizons, this horizon for example, to have to eat the fares, even the lesser fares, for metro and bus, the little trips to drink in paint, old or fresh, on canvas, to be so deprived, it isn't a riddle, no, all for the sake of a few measly books nobody buys, nobody wants to read, never to be able to call the tune, it isn't for her, and it strikes her, frankly, as silly, waiting to be dead to find out whether the few measly things will pluck up or plummet to oblivion. It does tend to go on food, on the necessities, if one is strapped for cash. The tummy rumbles, the hair has to be washed, the feet shod. Not to be able to spare a coin for a daily newspaper, to have to neglect one's health. No means for pleasure. Only misery. Only anxious.

Moreover, not for her the constant finger on unhappiness, on grief; let alone a hand-to-mouth life on top. One has to be fit to dredge grief up.

It is more honourable to generate the wherewithal and be a consumer, a happy consumer.

She's all admiration for the feeding of the fowls, in a kind of battery but laying such excellent eggs; and, with the sunshine on their batteries, the makeshift polythene sides lifted so they may enjoy a view out, they gurgle with contentment. The fowls have been supplied with proper amounts of grit and she'd like, dearly, to hear the secret of their feed. Yolks and whites enviable.

The sheep may have scrapie but otherwise they are taken out with a dog, the shepherd sleeps on a stone in the valley, the manager of the shop buys his cheese from farther afield. No suggestion that all the sheep in Israel have scrapie. The shepherd isn't an Arab.

To have to live with a single pair of shoes, could I live with a single pair of shoes.

Ah well, I am a man. It would pain her.

Arab children are said to torment cats and stone them, she hasn't herself had any opportunity to watch the stoning of cats, there aren't any Arabs in the village, only one or two who behave, the shepherd for instance, like Arabs, so she doesn't know how true it may be. It's possible it's true. There possibly is a gulf, in attitudes to animals, and some of us have swung against stoning. It's possible it's mythic.

She doesn't read men.

It isn't deliberate, it happens spontaneously. She doesn't, that's all. She gravitates in a bookshop towards the women, the women have something to say which is interesting, women speak.

On a table, or in a section of shelves.

... In literature apartheid then.

I am not to be daft.

Is she truly free from worry of money. She confesses she too thinks often of money, she has to drive herself to maintain the channels of supply.

I have a thought for Mozart.

After a while they grow on her, all these shining settlements in the sunlight, so many crusader castles, the Israelis march triumphant, white, upon the line of the sky. Arab villages were quietly tucked below it; deserted, they give her a perpetual sadness, she thinks Israelis don't see them any more.

She researches. She spent a month in Aigues-Mortes, in the winter-time. She goes to Jaffa. Now, it's Qastel. She walks to Qastel through the orchards.

In the crusades women were prominent. They were.

But there's been over the centuries a conspiracy to deny and conceal their role.

Her characters live with her. More real than I am, they prod her themselves in the right direction.

I can call it inspiration if I want. If I insist. She has no name for it. She and they are doing her job, and when the book is finished they will plummet into oblivion. She can forget them and they, they will live, with luck, once again in the heads of readers.

She thanks me for my courteous interest. I did express interest, didn't I.

She counts herself a talker. I myself less so . . . she presumes.

I shake my head. It isn't that.

It may be apocryphal, the cats tortured in the street, or at least stoned on a routine basis, so many things told her may be.

She pokes a finger under her fringe.

Fewer and fewer people in Europe know how to entice hens into laying nice eggs, equally fewer and fewer people can boil eggs, the two go together, if one can't boil an egg right it isn't because one is a poor cook, what is lacking is acquaintance with poultry and eggs. The freshness or staleness is crucial in boiling and timing the boil, and the size, it stands to reason, contributory.

Do I swim. The moshav has put a manager in the swimming pool. The deckchairs somehow disappear, each year he demands new, the moshav supplies deckchairs for the swimming pool as though distributing chicken feed. Then it is asked where its biblical zoo is, it has no biblical zoo, ah but it has, the manager has started one by the swimming pool, and reaps the profits himself.

It is known how many hens you have laying by how many eggs you produce, you are given so much feed for these so many fowls, you choose to sell your eggs in a free market, which isn't supposed to exist, you have to sell some eggs in the ordinary fashion so as to be in a position to feed the hens, you filter off a number of eggs because the price is more friendly to you, but the problem remains, how do you feed a hundred when it seems only sixty live with you in your battery houses.

You rear pullets or cockerels, or you have day-old chicks, whatever it is you do there comes a date at which they are developed, after which you will be feeding them pointlessly, they stand still, they eat your profit, so you have to have a chum at the passing-on-to-the-market end, you make a chum on purpose, the chum will see right other chums first, before you, if not; you are at their mercy; once one poultry-farmer makes a chum, once one person in the system allows herself or himself to be made into a chum, once fairness to all is in the soup, you are stuck with corruption. With human nature. The system sickens under the pressure. Though it remains in theory totally admirable, a system of some finesse.

The moshav is weighed down by debt, which cripples many emotionally, so they run away. So many high hopes and principles, then disappointment.

They know how to grow and rear things, the pork is excellent.

It can send one mad with grief, Israel. She wants to arrange how we are to meet.

... The shepherd nods off, sleeps an hour or two at a time, the dog decides it's a day, he'll take the flock home, he sets them very gently in motion, he eases them, letting them graze and day-dream and wander to and fro, he eases them towards the dam in the direction of home. The shepherd wakes: no sheep. The sheep, shepherded only by the dog, are already far off, the shepherd hollers, hollers again, or whistles, she doesn't think he whistles, he shouts, reluctantly the dog turns them and they drift back until the shepherd sits on his stone in their midst and the dog, abashed, lets its ears droop.

She is alienated by my dropping a scrap of paper. Not dropping, *chucking*. I screwed it up and it fell out of my fingers, litter, extraordinary, that I could, she is embarrassed but can't in the circumstances keep her mouth shut.

And suppose she does feel estranged, with regard to

animals, from the Palestinians, a *twinge* of estrangement, does the Torah spare a syllable on litter, did Jesus heal a donkey, could Jesus too plead thoughtlessness. She doesn't know.

Not so long ago Christians still pole-axed cattle and shelled horses. Nowadays they conceal their calluses.

Callousness.

In Aigues-Mortes, smoked horses for sale.

It's because horses are brave and intelligent. More sensitive than cloven-footed beasts.

Donkeys are sensitive but their minds work quite differently. The horizon in Jerusalem gives her a camel, led by a walking man.

The sky gives her biblical stars; the fields, orchids. The biblical sky at night and the biblical fields by day. In the wadi, stranded domestic machinery, car doors and sheets of tin, polythene is hitched up in the broom, stuff strewn beside the tracks, or into the water of the lake when there is water. Two boys sail a raft on it, not a leap-frog but touches her heart, romantic childhood adventures, ramshackle contrivances.

Her eyes can accommodate both almond blossom and rusty Israeli corrugated, the poppies and the concrete dam, cracked and unlovely, she sees only beauty, peace.

The searing, frog-leaping, in Palestine, almond blossom, the scent wafts in great billows and makes jelly of her, not sure if Berenice and Cecilia so susceptible.

Up to Qastel we climb.

I and she, with Berenice and Cecilia, the four of us, this late afternoon, peer down on to the road up to Jerusalem from the coast, Berenice and Cecilia will have disembarked at Jaffa, Tel Aviv not even a speck in someone's eye. Below Qastel linger memories, poignant too for Berenice and Cecilia, who know nothing of 1948. She chose the name Cecilia because it's with Cecilia she herself identifies rather. Cecilia isn't so far from Celia. By all means there can be men in the book but they are more shadowy.

She didn't say cardboard, it was shadowy she said. I don't understand, how could I. It's decent of me to try.

She's sorry to burden me with Berenice and Cecilia, they have to go with her, she with them, afraid it must be a riddle for me.

Berenice has put the Cross before her baby at home. For her the fever remains an option. It's sad! Books take hold, write themselves. Not a popular wisdom. Pretty true, they do. If Cecilia is to be left alone in Palestine. In the holy land.

With the holiness only in so far as it concerns Cecilia. The idea Cecilia has of infidels diverges severely from her own, but then Cecilia isn't a twentieth-century product.

Nor is Cecilia bothered over donkeys.

It's Berenice who is raped, not by an infidel, by a fellow crusader. The climax of the novel. Or one of them.

The fever, if she has it, shall be understated, in order to enhance the scenario. Berenice expires, if she is to, full of sang-froid, I can be sure.

Berenice's state of mind when raped is still an unknown. I am not to mock. She isn't offended. It's an education for me. They fill out like chickens. Then perhaps stuck, ha ha. Berenice and Cecilia aren't aware of me, they can't object to me, any more than they're aware of 1948. I can't in any case share in their emotion.

She reckons her title neat.

Women, crusade!

She has to, every day, if she doesn't she feels ill. Not quite like going to the lavatory, but not far off. Now there's a gift from the gods. She couldn't bear to be one of these sensitive, fragile souls who have to wake up one morning and find it all gone, their heads bereft, have to wait patiently, sometimes for years, blocked. It has never left her, her fluency. She would hate to have to protect herself, guard herself like a fortress, which is what you have to do if susceptible to being blocked, to have to be fearful when the telephone rings, or the postman comes, to have to steel yourself for eventualities, such tension wouldn't appeal to her at all, any more than it appeals to those who suffer it. She has no fortress mentality, her temperament is her strength.

To exist the whole time in either a trance or a state of disintegration.

She shakes her head, as if in disbelief. No, she wouldn't be a type like that for the world.

She doesn't have to be egg-bound with neuroses.

In her think-box, the almond breaks into blossom day after day, without fail.

Ah, never lonely, it's a friend. I probably remember childhood, with dreamed-up persons. It's so similar. No matter what she turns her hand to, she has an attendant, her own think-box.

Though now all green, yellow later; the crusaders will be seeing it dry, burnt; the valley, the wadi; but she has to go home, go from the holy land, so imagination comes into play.

I am to meet her tomorrow.

The donkeys, whether ... she walks with impunity in the Old City ... for jerry cans or a gross man, sport a strap, a cousin to the breeching in carriage-harness, under the quarters, to restrain the load, between, one might say, the hock and the tail, because it is adjusted up and down to avoid the sore of the day before, and the sore of several days previous, all donkeys in Palestine have sores in this place, some bad, some less bad, and she can't help but be disapproving.

The donkey's a difficult shape, she will grant. She does have sympathy, though not with the lack of gumption.

There is no need for the strap to rub.

She has no business, on the basis of her chancy experience, to weigh big questions up, isn't under a compulsion to know.

Cecilia, Berenice, they don't weigh, they do know; never hesitate, never question, they're quite, quite sure. They didn't disembark with open minds, theirs were closed. Unfortunately, a closed mind is more often than not a strength.

Since their day we ought to have advanced. Only one constant: men, and how they behave. Towards women.

Her two, since they have to take on men at their own game, are belligerent. The holy places, an added element. It is a holy war. However, we shouldn't imagine the crusaders spent all their time fighting and breaching fortifications and wading in blood, they spent ages sitting, strolling, having fevers and admiring the view.

Of course she does some research, why else was she in Aigues-Mortes last winter. She doesn't feel bound by facts. After all, what are facts. Facts are men's version of history, and at variance often with each other. In her *fiction*, a *truth*.

She isn't too bothered over what pretends to be accuracy. She isn't playing with history, men-historians have, men have played with it with outrageous arrogance. But she takes great care to get the feel. The feel's important. In the getting of it there are also delightful surprises.

Well, in this day and age a donkey train, twenty pack-donkeys. Or the biblical hoopoes.

It pretends to be a stupid bird, it seems to enjoy leap-frog over cats.

To whom does it matter, does it really matter if she can't herself tell the fourth crusade from the second, is anyone likely to suffer. She isn't thinking of modern distortions of history, who said she was.

Saladin has not yet taken back Jerusalem.

She has to check Cecilia, her own heart leap-frogs when she meets a wild tortoise. Cecilia's won't.

She's been to witness the shuttered face of the intifada, her strange privilege, to pass in the souk unseen, though people call out to her, it isn't necessary to tuck a Palestinian newspaper under her arm, or hold a map in her hand, she stares, she looks around, it is enough, her body says it, what she is, what she isn't.

She's aware each of us tells at a glance ... Her eye lit on the feet of a man in carpet slippers. Only Israelis wear carpet slippers to go around in. Only an Israeli mad enough to forget to change them for the Old City. Caked mud, little more than days ago, bedroom-slipper-dry, at the foot of the dam. If I must be technical, above. It deluges and suddenly a great wide stretch of water flies across the wadi. The dam is ugly. The water is far from ugly, and supplies her with endless pleasure. It will stay to let things hatch, it is a rich pond. Time enough to multiply the dragonflies, for the migrating storks to be magnetised out of the air. It isn't drinking water, it's soaking-away water, it is water for the ground, the earth, it soaks instead of pelting all the miles to the sea, it is a long-sighted idea so she tolerates the dam.

The flock crosses beneath the dam downstream: the half-naked sheep, their wool hanging in dirty biblical skeins.

One may safely reckon Berenice to have a sense of the horde. The cross shall thrust the horde back like the dog does the sheep, by force of conviction, with an air of unpunctured confidence.

She has to break the back of this chapter.

She wonders if the crusaders got in a lather about fecundity, families with twelve children, did the family with twelve children attain mythic proportions. Didn't I realise, am I not aware, Palestinians have twelve babies.

The bulbuls on the branches in the garden cuddle up like budgerigars. She suggests we make our rendezvous.

Well, the moshav debts are colossal. Inflation arrived. Idealism was punctured. Figures mount. Panic sets in. Woolly decisions were made, bad management introduced.

She's fond of mauve.

Brown and white, with venom very poisonous, in and out of the dead semi-submerged wood the sofer swims, you die in fifteen minutes flat. She can't allow Berenice to be, or Cecilia, but perhaps a man, definitely a man could be bitten. The scorpions small, no enormous harm, but a man could flump down on a scorpiony stone. She never has a man for a hero, utter cheek, bullshit, for men writers to commandeer the mind of a woman, it's for women alone to know how a woman would think. She knows, because women know how other women think, and feel. But that would do for a minor mishap. Crusaders tough.

She clasps her fingers behind her neck and chews her bottom lip.

The moshav has let the shop slip, a person comes in and runs it for himself. The moshav gives it into his hands for a tiny rent on condition he keeps the prices modest, for the benefit of those in the village, the members. He doesn't keep his prices down at all, he sits on the shop and makes a fat profit for himself and his sons. The moshav begs that he pay increased rent, he replies, no, end of the matter. He is still sitting on the shop and he and his idle sons grow richer.

Berenice can't, in the village, smile at the Arab workmen who are waiting to catch the bus. Berenice doesn't see Palestinian workmen. No, or the bus. Neither does Cecilia. Israelis, people who name themselves after poisonous snakes and fearsome plants of the desert, thorns, they don't see them either.

The writeress does, and receives a radiant look.

Her valley, the old ruins of houses, different centuries, the old road, beside which the mulberry-trees, who sees it, you would imagine no one could avoid it, picturing it as it once was. And in the forest, the terraces climb the hill still beneath the trees, the forest like a sacred grove, memorials to diaspora Jews scattered where once Palestinians broke their backs tilling soil and growing things, Yad Vashem now sits on the heads and backs of all these Palestinian spectres. It makes her think. One needs trees, forests, though. And if not here, where, a sacred grove has rights too.

She doesn't understand, I appear to indicate.

The old ruins up there too. And Yad Vashem looks down on dinosaur footprints.

Her pulli she bought in the Aigues-Mortes market.

If one were to see the old road along the wadi, the old stones, how would one stifle them, qualms. If not oblivious to little houses one shoots past every day, even though no one has lived in them for centuries.

Nor do the Orthodox, converging on the Western Wall, see *her*, they don't look where they're going and bump into people, Israelis say the Orthodox bump into people, into women, that is, on purpose, they mustn't see but they let themselves bump. With thoughts on prayers one may bump with impunity; one can't have eyes in the back of one's head.

One does try not to be bumped, very often the collision will be at a tangent. Pity I can't go with her to the Temple Mount. The beauty palpable, it's to do with the spaces, the stones, the stones speak. Not fanatic hordes but streams of calm human beings fill the tiny streets of the Old City after the Friday prayers.

It's important to voice it, all of it, I voice nothing, she fears she offends, we all offend, it's our tenuous hold on truth; no risk, no truth; I raise my brows, do I; no risk of offending, all deception. How easy it is to patronise the patronised.

But which was the horde, Mohammedan or crusader.

She doesn't know if crusaders intrigued by fossils, she'll give it a think. She thanks me. The terracing is how old, that's the real question in her mind. Does it pre-date the bent-double Palestinians. She feels in her bones it must do.

The rape of Berenice might be on a dinosaur's footprint, or do I consider that too fantastic. Hot-blooded, many incensed leap-frogs. She as its creator, however, cold, can discuss it with detachment.

She is ticklish.

She was once in a cottage some woodlice counted their own, it might have been a wood-shed in Berenice's time and the memory of the louse is tenacious, or perhaps a simple plague, to start with one treats them tenderly, all the woodlice in her bedroom she told to roll up in a ball and be transported in the hollow of a piece of paper. It's an inoffensive creature, isn't disgusting, isn't dirty, goes about its business. It rarely hops into bed with one. It gives a wholesome crunch if stepped on in the dark, even bare feet aren't revolted. A spider specialises in paralysing the woodlouse and sucking all the goodness out. If one cultivates such a spider in one's bedroom, one finds the shells of the corpses all over the place. But the spider's life is the more fragile in a house of vacuum-cleaners and dusters, baby woodlice can continue to appear relentless. The vacuum-cleaner brings them out of the cracks, like vibration worms beside the motorway. But belatedly; and to clean twice, worry about them in the belly of the machine, is consuming. Tapped with the shoe the woodlouse readies itself to be kicked. Circumspect kicks will oblige it to arrive outside. It flies the stairs thanks to its armour undamaged. The more tiresome uncurl before the end of their journey and have to be re-tapped. The adolescent don't have perfected reflexes, and their backs are made of softer stuff. Also, small for kicking, it's a job to get them rolling, one has to aim the kick so as to loft them into the air, and the risk to their persons is greater. Nevertheless, with patience ... It becomes borne on one that the woodlice are too many, irritation with them mounts, no spider around to suck at them, they're no longer picturesque, solemnly trundling about their business, but a horde, an invasion. The kicking foot is less circumspect. The woodlice seem a little re-pulsive, after all. One woodlouse does hop into bed. The kick becomes vicious. The woodlice haven't changed in character a jot, they have multiplied, and are intolerable. It is the character of the kick which has changed.

To help me: the louse is an armadillo with more legs and minus snout.

It is a woodlouse, not a louse. Would one take a louse to the door on a piece of paper, now!

Is it likely she'd kick a louse downstairs.

Her stories aren't far-fetched.

To the other side of Jerusalem the desert wind is moaning. Palpable always, always. Her valley, no whistles or howls; it's a quiet valley and she never wants to leave it.

To start with, we kill cleanly.

Quite kind, we are, to one rat, to one cockroach, we smile at one rat, rats look hateful only when they are too many, their appearance changes, cockroaches also look hateful, yet to one hateful on its own compassion is in order, not ruthlessness.

Vermin, did he. Did they. She didn't know. Oh.

. . . Orchids are so fragile. One may find terraces which climb up beneath fir plantations, or are abandoned, in many spots, in Europe, but not so poignantly.

The white knuckles clenched already on the sky-line, and in the valley eight different orchids.

It is possibly her favourite, at the moment, walk in the world, the path along the fringe of the Jerusalem forest, to En Karem, no doubt the Baptist toddled as a child where we are putting our great hooves, well some doubt, because one can't be sure of anything, and saw the same green mouths of the lizards, the same poppies.

If we're puffed we can stop and sit. We are to turn our feet, and stagger over the slabs of rock.

Haven't I eyes in my head . . .

I stepped straight over a dinosaur's footprint.

She teases, it is only after one knows how to recognise the dinosaur that one treads with attention.

It is petrified mud, she supposes. In those days they were stumping beside the sea.

That one can meet a dinosaur's footprint on an ordinary stroll, or the wild cyclamen, the white light of day and the biblical sky by night, all, the sunbirds and the bulbul, the scent of the almond blossom and the fluttering of the plum, old stones, it has ravished her mind, she stands in the Old City, or up by the Hebrew University, looking down on the Dead Sea far away, towards the desert, *into* the desert, and she thinks she will never recover.

They look to her like the prints of the pterodactyl, that is what leaps to the imagination. In the cool of the forest.

The Palestinians ran away from En Karem, their leaders told them, run away now and in three or four days we'll come back and kill all the Jews, so although the attacking force was composed of sixteen year olds the Palestinians ran away and the sixteen year olds, a brigade of them, attacking from three sides, found pots on the fire and the smell of cooking, everything dropped, the Palestinians never came back, she supposes it's true, fatal to run away.

The hold seems fragile, illusory, so easy to repulse, to thrust it all, dream or nightmare, us from our present perch on the petrified mud, to Jaffa.

It's fatal to run away, but sometimes one has to.

Or shall Jerusalem roll over eight orchids and the dinosaurs' feet, gleaming, all the way to the sea.

Ran away, after which they each had twelve babies.

The almonds are long set and nuts green.

... Her shoes are stained by olives squished in the dark, the juice spurts up her legs.

Palestinians used to buy the tree's whole crop. But Arabs cheat and it wasn't worth the irritation.

Jews brought up among Arabs will tell you what they think you want to hear and not the truth. One *doesn't* say it any more; yet it floats out of the lips quite often.

She has her ear to the ground.

Listening to her is to listen to the street, I listen to her and hear the street.

Her blouse has popped a button.

Human beings are still human beings. One can thumb a lift and cars will stop, strangers, sweet people, and one can climb in and it is safe.

I wouldn't understand how unsafe at home, in the land of the woodlouse, unsafe and in fact impossible, like the ignoring of an unattended parcel in the Jerusalem Bus Station would be.

She pities my ignorance, because it is plain I am due to find out, I am in for a disappointment.

In the land of the woodlouse, children can't play in country lanes, can't be alone, so many women are raped, ninety and stuck in bed, so many babies starved to death, tormented, so much buggery of tiny tots, so many rich, so many poor, so much ideology, swallowed by those, indeed, who would profess themselves *anti* her, la dame de fer.

I may suppose I can say really! really! in that tone of voice but I've no notion. Thousands in cardboard boxes night after night on the pavement or in concrete underpasses, old folk tipped out on to the street, and the ill, the unbalanced, even the poor insane.

Better wipe it off my face.

I talk with reverence, positive reverence, of literature, of art, well it all hinges, in the louse land, on money, on earning power, on elbows and gumption, and fibs.

And she's still there, making them resentful.

I imagine it is so free, do I. They too have censorship, a form of it, very subtle, and a big mansion, shining and innocent as a babe, for telephone-tapping.

I may well look amazed, have I fondly thought, no telephone-tapping.

True, she hasn't taken their whole lives, their grown-up lives, true. Not yet.

I may be not an unborn babe, but Berlin isn't London or New York, West Berlin isn't *real*. I may read newspapers, I may not be clueless, granted. One can learn swiftly.

I can't learn too swiftly, I should wake up. If I think she

invents stories about people asleep in boxes I've another think coming.

Democracy, ah, a hit-and-miss affair, no utopia, rather fallible. So many democratic rights chopped from under their feet of late.

Ooops, I have an inkling, have I, she does, does she, exaggerate, I've been about, have I, well I mustn't be put out by her snorting so.

Berenice and Cecilia wouldn't recognise it! In their day a different loutishness. They didn't have television.

The sight of the face always, hearing the voice, it makes one sick and disgusted. It's beyond me to imagine, she supposes.

One pays the rabbi not to ask about periods, when one wants a marriage done. Might we not arrange to meet, what have we got on.

No mulberry-trees in the Bible, she thinks the crusaders brought it.

Those are they, follow her finger.

Ho, I fancy otherwise, do I. They're biblical as well, are they.

Berenice and Cecilia will have it in their pockets, all the same; and the cornflower is sown by their horses, the crusaders exemplary as far as flora is concerned.

Of course one can be quite unclothed and secretly menstruating.

I must forgive her for laughing. She expects they've made advances denied to us.

The Arabs, people tell her, with their twenty-one countries, they have the pick of twenty-one. Or twenty-two, it varies, countries, they attacked, they were *conquered*.

Sometimes she's lonely.

Did she really say she's never lonely.

When Berenice and Cecilia abandon her.

We are all lonely, all alienated, all lost, I mustn't think myself unique, all displaced.

The rights of sorrow, sorrow too has rights.

The Palestinians in the Old City tell her, it is hard, we try to bring them to their senses, so as to have our life a little less oppressive, a little, that's all, ameliorated.

Stones kill. She wants to break into my thoughts.

There is no such word as writeress.

Oh well a donkey like all donkeys, with a mind of its own, and the easily-wounded pride of the humble, little stick legs, a thin old lady's or a gazelle's, and narrow quarters, was tied up at a door in the Old City with its nose, her nose, two inches from the wall, her head and neck fixed like a nail, uncomfy at the best of times, excruciating after jerry cans, or the overweight man, why is it, by the by, overweight men are those most attracted to donkeys, the donkey needs to relax its whole body and can't, if not cruelty tantamount to great unkindness, probably not vicious, at least probably not, no *imagination*, no regard for donkey, physically or mentally, poor donkey, it longs to drop its head a bit and let the tension run out of its body.

The reasoning is clear.

If she were to swing about at will on a longer rope she might bump tourists with her hind-end, block a hand-cart. Presented with a door, a wall and a ring or old hinge or whatever, the master, like the young outnumbered soldiers, hasn't a lot of scope, he can't rely on her to hug the cool of the wall, she might take it into her head to fidget, and particularly if half tired, if dead tired she might wilt on the spot. Given she has to stay put while her master, the overweight man, is inside.

One feels distaste, one's immediate reaction is to recoil.

One has only to lay eyes on a Palestinian donkey, for sympathy to start to ebb.

She, naturally, had sores in the usual places, and nasty enough for flies to sit on, eat.

I'd have noticed nothing amiss and walked on by.

She walked on by too.

It stabs the heart, with exasperation; and one's impression is coloured disagreeably.

It is also silly, of the master, though he can't appreciate that, poor master, because whilst she is tied so close to the wall, a form of torture, inside she seethes, two inches of free rope, inadvertent or not, creates a resentful donkey, less likely to be obedient, to do what it's told with a good grace; let alone live longer.

A jenny donkey is soon humiliated.

No loosening of girths.

The difficulty is, what, after one has walked on by, has one really seen.

Has the donkey been tied up for two minutes or two hours.

If two minutes, no great harm done.

But if for two minutes she might have been allowed more rope, the chances are, in a quiet street, she would have hindered no one, added local colour for the tourists, these days few enough of those, and those incapable of squeezing past a donkey can jolly well retrace their steps, a jenny most unlikely to molest a tourist, besides it's doubtful if tourists were the true concern.

Is there perhaps a law in Jerusalem regarding donkeys' hind-quarters, dominion over them.

If for two hours, horrid.

Ignorance doesn't relieve one of responsibility and is in some sense chosen.

Lofty, well, innocence, would I prefer.

Innocence.

But then, what of our civilised barbarity, she has to come back to it, we don't kill the pig we fatten, and they don't kill pigs at all, or fatten them, in the land of the woodlouse one no longer knows how to kill, kindly or unkindly, at home one's eye doesn't meet so many beasts of burden, at home they're starved to death because people imagine they eat stinging nettles in a pocket handkerchief, and all those buggered toddlers, all of us trip up.

One can't be sure of anything. Alas.

A donk's head, what goes on in it, can be very tiresome, it takes patience, to indulge all that goes on in a jenny's think-box, it's almost a gift. But replace the overweight man with a woman, then some hope; with men, and their putting of their legs over, no hope, stagnation.

Our eyes, because bung full of prejudice, see what isn't there to see.

What if our brains were to telephone our eyes and whisper that the Palestinians treat their donkeys with more consideration than we do ours, would the sores disappear.

So one hunts for a Palestinian donkey with no sores or rubbed places, and what if one can't find such a beast, one has to think of women . . . no, no *evidence* that women are better, I am not to make her grind her teeth . . . think of women, and look, for the donkey, to the future. One mustn't go around sampling cultures. The offered food.

She isn't sure Israel should be here at all, am I sure.

The boat has been to En Gedi, for an afternoon. The bathers lie on the water as if in deckchairs, so it is true; and laugh, with white teeth, the strange teeth of tourists. One cannot go so low and still see the sky, it is the lowest place on earth. It is very beautiful and very disgusting.

They don't kiss hands, they kiss each other's bottoms a lot though.

It seems one can look out over the Dead Sea and feel irredeemably desolate. Its hot breath, the shores caked in salt ... but no slime pits, no slime pits visible, no bitumen erupted whilst she was there. I should not enjoy it. And it's plain if one stands too near for too long one will be coated. One gropes for the pebbles, their ravishing colours, the pebbles tremble to and fro, and one's hands, dipped, are withdrawn all sticky and nasty.

Do I really imagine she doesn't crave. Behind every brave face probably something sadder. The Judean hills sit, so quiet, over one's shoulder. They shimmered uneasily under her gaze ...

She uses her elbows in bed, she cultivates them. So many sharp elbows in the land of the woodlouse, apparently. Israel a gentle country.

So many things to surprise one, how, after they've shaken hands, they like to eye one and jump in, it is fairly rapid, they wouldn't deign to dissemble, dissimulate, it's a point of honour, though I am not slow, if I am not slow why on earth should she be, can I please tell her that. To her I am a bird in the garden, slightly exotic, and quaint. She supposes my purity, acquired through my isolation in a totalitarian system, is a gift I hand someone.

I think: we pretend a kind of weary pleasure. One may be desolate and still there is exquisite sensation. So one day we can make love to someone who smells, or whose breath is tainted. Hand over our gift of freedom from the *sida*. Eager, willing, for the flesh to creep.

Each with our thoughts.

So much one doesn't say, we edge round the great silences.

A joy and agony, as if the mind were blind with tears.

Too many memories, too much sensibility. And this woman, telling me where to put my bulbul.

She's been eating fish.

I left her and took the bus to Tel Aviv and walked like the dinosaurs to and fro by the sea. Helplessly alone. I was to taste from then on with the furry tongue of a creature dead, in me something had already died, there would be no more joy, no more agony.

Poor dinosaurs, to and fro glumly by the frill of the sea, out of puff, or swaying with their little withered elbows in the air down Dizengoff Street.